# Land of Promise

## MERIDIAN LINES

(INCORPORATED)

## LANDING CARD

(THIRD CLASS PASSENGERS)

Manifest Sheet No. *17*

*Name*

*Rose Carney*

*List Number* **8**

ELLIS ISLAND

# Land of Promise

❖ ❖ ❖

## JOAN LOWERY NIXON

A BANTAM SKYLARK BOOK
NEW YORK · TORONTO · LONDON · SYDNEY · AUCKLAND

LAND OF PROMISE
A Bantam Book / May 1993
The Starfire logo is a registered trademark of Bantam Books, a
division of Bantam Doubleday Dell Publishing Group, Inc.
Registered in U.S. Patent and Trademark Office and elsewhere.

Library of Congress Cataloging-in-Publication Data

Nixon, Joan Lowery.
Land of promise / by Joan Lowery Nixon.
p. cm.—(Ellis Island novel ; #2)
Summary: In 1902 fifteen-year-old Rose travels from Ireland
to join family members in Chicago, where she must use all her
resources to deal with her father's drinking and her brothers'
dangerous involvement in politics.
ISBN 0-553-08111-X
[1. Irish Americans—Fiction. 2. Chicago (Ill.)—Fiction. 3.
Emigration and immigration—Fiction.] I. Title. II. Series:
Nixon, Joan Lowery. Ellis Island novel ; #2.
PZ7.N65Lap 1993
[Fic]—dc20                                            92-28591
                                                          CIP
                                                          AC
Published simultaneously in the United States and Canada

Bantam Books are published by Bantam Books, a division of Bantam Doubleday Dell Publishing Group, Inc. Its trademark, con-
sisting of the words "Bantam Books" and the portrayal of a
rooster, is Registered in U.S. Patent and Trademark Office and in
other countries. Marca Registrada. Bantam Books, 1540 Broad-
way, New York, New York 10036.

PRINTED IN THE UNITED STATES OF AMERICA
BVG        0  9  8  7  6  5  4  3  2  1

*In loving memory
of my paternal grandparents
Mary Elizabeth Murphy Lowery
and
Peter Lowery
who emigrated to the United States
from Ireland*

# CHAPTER ONE

❖ ❖ ❖

ROSE Carney snatched up her skirts with one hand
and ran as fast as she could down the path that led
from the Ellis Island inspection station to the New Jersey
ferry as its whistle gave two long, sharp blasts.

Her friend Kristin Swensen and her parents had already
joined the line of immigrants who had passed the dreaded
physical and mental examinations and would enter the
United States through Jersey City, hub of the railroad
lines that led to many distant parts of the United States.
Muttering to herself, Rose hurried to catch up with the
Swensens while at the same time she tried to keep her
wicker suitcase from bumping against her legs and throwing her off balance.

Rose was furious with her uncle Jimmy for deserting
her at the immigration station. She'd counted on traveling
with him to Chicago, where they'd join her father and

1

two older brothers, but Uncle Jimmy had abruptly broken the news that he was staying in New York.

"You're a big girl, almost grown," he'd told her as he tucked a railway ticket into her hands, "and perfectly able to travel to Chicago by yourself."

As Uncle Jimmy disappeared through the door that led to the New York ferries, there'd been no time for Rose to tell him just what she thought. Now, as she rushed toward the ferry, she grumbled through a dozen angry I-should-have-saids.

"I can't believe I have to make the trip to Chicago alone!" she told the Swensens as she tried to catch her breath.

She heard the tremor of fear in her voice and, trying to get herself in hand, silently scolded herself. *You're not a child, Rosie Carney. You were frightened when you left Liverpool for the United States on that great whale of a ship, but you made the voyage without mishap. And there's no reason why you can't join your father in Chicago still in one piece.*

As the ferry chugged away from the dock, Kristin sat down and patted a place for Rose. "You won't be alone," she said with a smile. "Father told me we'll be traveling with you all the way to Chicago."

"How could that be?" Rose asked. "You're going to Minnesota, not Chicago."

"Look at your ticket. It says the Chicago, Milwaukee and St. Paul Railway," Kristin explained, and laughed at Rose's loud sigh of relief.

Rose lowered her voice even though Mr. and Mrs. Swensen had made their way through the crowd of passengers to the rail and were watching the massive, towered, red-and-yellow brick building on Ellis Island recede into the distance. "I can't help worrying about meeting my father again," she confided. "It's been almost four years since he left Ireland, and I was only a girl of twelve. What if he doesn't recognize me?" Rose swallowed hard, then continued, "I confess that even though Ma had an old photograph of him, taken when he was young, sometimes it's hard to remember his face. What if *I* don't recognize *him*?"

"You'll find each other with no trouble," Kristin assured Rose. "Take off your kerchief, and that red hair of yours will be like a beacon light flashing: Here's Rose! Here's Rose!"

Rose couldn't keep from smiling. "I wish that Da could have afforded to bring Ma and my younger sisters to the United States with me. I've never before, in almost sixteen years, been separated from my mother." A little enviously she added, "You and Rebekah are lucky that your families could come to the United States together."

"You said there'd be enough money to send for your mother and sisters in two years. That's not so long," Kristin said, but her voice lacked conviction.

"It *is* a long time," Rose insisted.

Her eyes burned with tears as she pictured Ma, Bridget, and Meggie on the Liverpool docks nearly three weeks before. She fought back the tears, twisting to peer at the receding New York skyline, forcing herself to think of anything else.

"I hope that all goes well for Rebekah and her family," Rose managed. "New York City seems so crowded. I hear it's a terrifying place. I wouldn't want to live there."

"It must be exciting," Kristin said. "I think I'd like to

live in a city. Life can be awfully dull on a farm." She gave Rose a careful look. "Chicago's a big city, too. My father said so."

Rose shivered and drew her shawl more closely around her shoulders. "Much like Dublin, I suppose, and I'm not a bit comfortable in Dublin with all its noise and horses and carts and people hurrying along the streets when they aren't packed into buildings like eggs in a crate."

"I think Rebekah will be happy living in New York City," Kristin said, "because she wants an education, and a city has schools."

Rose ached as she thought about Rebekah, the other friend she had made on board the ship. Befriending Kristin and Rebekah had made the dreadful voyage in steerage bearable; although their lives and futures were so different, the girls felt as though they'd been friends for years. Rose hated the fact that they'd had to part.

"Do you really think that one day the three of us will be together again?" Rose asked.

"I *know* we will." Kristin nodded emphatically. "I believe in making things happen."

The ferry bumped against the dock, and many of the passengers snatched up their belongings, pushing and shoving toward the gangplank.

"Stand back! Move aside!" the crew yelled as they slung lines to the dock, then jumped down to swiftly pull from the ship the attached hawsers, dropping their heavy loops around the mushroom-shaped bits that rose from the dock.

Mr. Swensen, who was taller and broader shouldered than most of the other men on board, had no trouble shepherding his family down the short gangplank onto the dock. Kristin reached out a hand and dragged Rose along.

They walked to the nearby railway station, which was crowded with passengers.

"Look at that gentleman with his top hat and gold-tipped cane," Kristin whispered to Rose, but Rose was more interested in the bright posters tacked on the posts and walls throughout the station.

"California—Cornucopia of the World," one of them read. "Room for Millions of Immigrants." Rose continued reading, "43,795,000 Acres of Government Lands Untaken. A Climate for Health and Wealth without Cyclones or Blizzards."

Another touted Texas over the crowded eastern states, and a third poster announced that Kansas was the "Golden Belt Country."

Mr. Swensen, who had gone ahead to inquire about their train, elbowed his way back through the crowd, beaming. "Hear what they say about Minnesota: 'One immense empire of mineral, timbered, and agricultural wealth, waiting only to be occupied.' Was I not right to bring us here?"

Mrs. Swensen nodded yes, but Kristin said, "Pappa, we can't be sure until we arrive and see for ourselves."

Still smiling, Kristin's father answered, "We will soon be on our way to discovering the answer. Come. This way. Our train will leave in less than an hour."

"How long will it take to get to Chicago?" Rose asked.

"Chicago is around eight hundred and fifty miles or so. It will take a little more than two days and nights—we'll arrive the morning of the third day."

Nearly three days! Rose had not thought about where Chicago was located. It would be a long journey. She was again furious with her uncle. She'd left everything up to him. She was even more grateful to be with the Swensens.

"Let's move on now," said Mr. Swensen. Mrs. Swensen and Kristin hurried after him, Rose straggling along in the rear with her heavy suitcase.

Suddenly Rose felt a tug on her suitcase and whirled to see a smiling young man who was trying to pry her fingers from the handle of the case. With his free hand he tipped his cap and said, "I'll carry this for you, miss."

"I thank you, but I can carry the case myself," Rose told him.

The man's grip didn't loosen. "I'm no fool. If you think you've found a way to steal my belongings, then you've made a big mistake," Rose announced.

He tugged, but Rose was faster and kicked with all her strength at his shins. Then she balled her fist and smashed it into the bridge of his nose.

As the man let out a yell and jumped back, he released the suitcase and grabbed at his bleeding nose. Rose clutched her suitcase against her chest and used it as a ram to open a path through the milling passengers as she scurried after her traveling companions who were now up ahead.

Rose and the Swensens entered one of the railway cars for those who had paid lower fares and stowed their belongings and the packages of food they had purchased for the trip under the hard wooden seats. Rose and Kristin huddled together, noses pressed against the window.

Before long the train reached stretches of open country, and the tracks wound through rolling hills, past stands of aspen and pine, birch and maple. Scatterings of small yellow-and-white wildflowers appeared as bright surprises, and the large fields on the occasional farms they passed were pale green with newly sprouted seedlings.

"Look at the size of the farms!" Rose exclaimed. "These must all belong to titled landowners."

"There are no titles in the United States." Kristin giggled. "It's a democracy."

Rose laughed, too. "There's not a farmer in Ireland with more than a dollop of this much land. Only the wealthy English who stole the Irish estates have farms like these."

Kristin raised one eyebrow. "Stole?"

"Stole," Rose said firmly, "along with deroofing our churches, destroying our forests, and killing our game. For years the Irish were not even allowed to go to school, so some of them—like my parents—learned in secrecy to read and write."

"That's terrible!" Kristin exclaimed.

"Terrible—yes! But someday Ireland will be ours again."

"Are you talking about war?"

"May heaven protect us, I hope there'll be no war with its maimings and killings!" Rose shuddered as she said, "A man on the farm next to us was caught in the Clan na Gael bombings in Britain in the eighties. He was left blinded, and his face was so horribly disfigured from his burns that little children run in terror when they see him coming. Ma says that peaceful discussion is the only answer, not violence, and I agree with Ma. My brothers

7

and father talk about rousting the English by force. I love Ireland, but sometimes I'm frightened to think of what might happen."

"You don't have to be frightened here. This is America," Kristin said, and for a moment the two girls were silent, looking out at the farmland.

"In Ireland we lived on a farm," Rose said, and her throat tightened as memories filled her mind. "Our house was small, with a thatched roof, but the peat-burning stove and the fireplace kept it snug and warm. On cold nights Ma would heat bricks in the ashes and wrap them in towels, then tuck them in our beds to warm our toes."

Kristin nodded. "We had foot warmers, too."

"For a while we had three cows—now only one—and I'd lead them down the lane and over the hill to graze by the lake," Rose said. "Any neighbors who were working their crops would straighten and wave, maybe even come over to lean on the fence for a moment to chat." She smiled. "Old Mrs. O'Malley, may she rest in peace, always had a bit of gossip to pass along."

"Our neighbors in Sweden never stopped their work to talk," Kristin said, "but we all met at the Lutheran church each Sunday, and there were dinners and festivals. We had socials at our school, too."

"But no dances, you told us."

"That's right. Our pastor didn't approve. He was very strict, and when he hit the edge of his desk with his stick even the worst boys in class paid attention." She giggled and turned to Rose. "But I liked school. I really did. Did you?"

"Yes," Rose answered. "I went to school at the convent in Drogheda. Sister Rita was probably as strict as your pastor, but she was generous with praise and hugs. She begged us all to go on to higher education when we reached the age of fourteen, but how could we? None of us could afford it. The few secondary schools were in the cities."

"Cities offer so much that people living on farms can't have," Kristin said.

Rose smiled. "I'm the one who'll be living in a city, and you'll be on a farm. It seems as though we'd gladly change places."

Kristin's sigh was her only answer as she pressed her nose against the dusty glass window and stared out at the countryside.

As the train chugged across the state of Pennsylvania and through upper Ohio and Indiana, the hard benches and the constant swaying and lurching were uncomfortable. At each stop passengers would scramble down the steps, eager to move about and stretch sore muscles. Some depots served hot food, but those travelers who ran inside to order complained later that the service was so slow they had barely been served before the whistle on the train blew long blasts to signal its departure.

Rose was content with the chunks of bread, cheese, salted ham, and apples that Mrs. Swensen had packed, gladly paying her share of the cost to Mr. Swensen, even though Kristin muttered embarrassed remarks about it.

Although she was stiff from trying to sleep sitting up on the hard seats, Rose perked up as a porter walked through their car early the third morning and announced, "We've crossed into Illinois. We'll be in Chicago shortly."

Rose and Kristin hurried to the washroom at the end

of the car, where they scrubbed their arms and faces in the small basin and brushed their hair.

Rose tied a clean kerchief over her hair and studied her reflection in the mirror. She was no longer a twelve-year-old girl; she was grown, nearly a woman. Da would be surprised at how she had changed. But he would have changed, too. Was his hair still thick and black? His shoulders as broad and strong? She squeezed her eyes shut, trying to picture her father, Peter Carney, as she had last seen him, but she saw only a blur.

The jolting of the train threw her off balance, and she grabbed Kristin for support.

"You look fine," Kristin told Rose. "Now hurry. We want to look out the windows and see as much of Chicago as we can."

They squeezed past the conductor and the people around him who shouted in a variety of languages.

A short, plump woman pushed a card at Rose. Rose read what was printed on the card: *To the Conductor: Please show bearer where to change trains and where to get off, as this person does not speak English. Bearer is bound to Chicago, Illinois.* Underneath was the name of a civic league for immigrants.

Rose smiled and nodded. "We are coming into Chicago," she said slowly.

The woman grasped the one word she understood. "Chicago?" she echoed.

"Yes." Rose nodded and pointed to herself. "Chicago. I'm going to Chicago, too. I'll tell you when we get there."

The woman took her seat, but she kept her eyes on Rose.

As she sat next to Kristin, Rose murmured, "Another good-bye. First Rebekah, and now you."

"We're friends. We'll write," Kristin said emphatically. "We'll see each other again." But tears ran down her cheeks, and she buried her face against Rose's shoulder.

The train began to slow. As Rose held Kristin tightly, she saw that they were passing clusters of buildings, their dark-red brick covered with layers of soot. *Leonard Seed Company, Platt's Oysters* . . . tracks and more tracks . . . open grain cars on sidings . . . until finally the train crawled, ducking under a covered shed, and stopped, its brakes squealing loudly.

The plump woman pecked at Rose's shoulder. "Chicago?" she asked.

"Yes, Chicago," Rose answered. She struggled to her feet and gave Kristin one last hug. "Don't forget to send me your address as soon as you have one."

She shook hands with Mr. Swensen, but Mrs. Swensen cupped Rose's face with her hands and examined it. "You are pale," she said. "Do you feel ill?"

"No," Rose said and took a deep breath. "The truth is I'm more than a bit nervous about seeing my father again."

"Will he be here to meet you?"

"No," Rose said, "but I have his address. I'm certain there'll be plenty of good-hearted people who will help me find my way." She wished she felt as brave as her words. Her stomach hurt and it was hard to breathe, but she realized there was only one thing to do—leave the train and find her father's home.

Rose hoisted her suitcase and descended the steps of the railway car. From the wooden platform, Rose glanced at the steepled and gabled dark-brick station toward which the other passengers were hurrying. She followed them, pushed open a heavy door, and found herself in a massive, crowded, high-ceilinged room.

Rose looked for the woman who had asked her for help and was glad to see that she was surrounded by four tall young men who happily greeted her. When it was Ma's turn to come she'd get a royal welcome, too.

But there was no one to meet Rose, and standing in the station gawking at the people around her wouldn't accomplish anything. "Please, sir," Rose called to a uniformed man who was striding past, "could you tell me where I . . ."

"Sorry," he called over his shoulder as he kept going, "Got some folks waiting for a porter."

Someone jostled her, and Rose staggered off balance. She regained her footing and looked around indignantly, but the person had gone. "Without so much as an apology," Rose muttered to herself.

She made her way across the room and out the main doors onto the sidewalk. Carts and buggies passed at a steady clip, and an electric cable car rattled through the traffic. Draymen yelled at their horses, cab drivers shouted for passengers, and the hubbub was deafening.

Dublin was bad, but Chicago in 1902 was worse. Oh, if she could only go home and be with her mother and little sisters again!

# CHAPTER TWO

❖ ❖ ❖

As a hand gripped Rose's shoulder and spun her around, she shrieked and made a fist, but a grinning young man shouted, "Rosie, girl! It's me! Johnny!"

"Oh, Johnny! I'm that glad to see you!" Rose cried. She dropped her suitcase and wrapped her arms around her brother's neck, clinging tightly. "I didn't know who to ask for help. I didn't know where to go."

She released her grip and stepped back, looking into his face. Johnny was more handsome than ever, with his laughing eyes and the dimple that flickered in his chin. Well dressed in a dark suit, stiff collar, and cravat, he wore a derby tilted rakishly over one eye. Nineteen now, wasn't he? "You're a wonder," Rose said. "How did you know I'd be here?"

"Don't give him any credit. Your uncle sent a telegram with the information."

13

Rose noticed with surprise the tall, dark-haired young man about Johnny's age who'd been standing off to one side. He smiled—a smile almost as charming as Johnny's—and said, "I'm Timothy Ryan, Miss Rose Carney, and I came at your brother's request to help him pick up and deliver what he called his 'tag-along little sister.' "

"How'd I know you'd grown up, Rosie?" Johnny protested.

"I'm sorry you were put to the trouble, Mr. Ryan," Rose said. "As for Johnny . . ."

"Call me *Tim,* not Mr. Ryan," Tim said, and his smile deepened. "And please believe me, I'm *very* glad I came."

Rose was glad, too, and on the cable-car rides—they had to transfer twice—she enjoyed being tucked between the two men, listening to their good-natured banter, sometimes being included.

Tim teased Johnny about his political ambitions being even greater than those of the alderman for whom they worked. Rose smiled, although the things they talked about were so new to her. "I get the feeling that you like living in Chicago," she said.

"Like it?" Tim shrugged. "It's as good a place as any in this country, but it can't compare to home." For a moment anger flashed in his eyes and he said, "Would any of us have left Ireland if the alternative hadn't been starvation?"

Rose nodded. "It was terribly hard to leave, knowing I'd never see the country again."

"I didn't feel that way," Tim said, "because I *knew* I'd be back."

"You're going back? When?"

"Soon, I hope," Tim said. "When we have enough to

14

make it worthwhile." He looked over Rose's head to Johnny.

"I don't understand," Rose told him.

"We'll talk about it later." Johnny took Rose's hand and jerked her to her feet. "Here's our stop," he said and led her from the electric trolley across the dusty street to the sidewalk and over one block. A row of closely built, three-story wooden houses stretched down both sides of the street. They were almost identical, with steep stairways leading over half-buried first stories up to small porches and front doors.

"Isn't it fine?" Johnny said as he led the way to the fourth house on the right. "We've got a flat all to ourselves, and close to the trolley line."

Inside the house was another stairway leading to the top floor, but Johnny bypassed it, pulled out a key, and opened the front door to their flat.

"Who lives up there?" Rose asked.

"The O'Brien family," Johnny answered, "and even though this is mostly an Irish neighborhood, there's a Polish family—the Horbowys—below stairs. Nice people. You'll have no trouble with any of them."

People on top, people below. Rose felt strange, as though she were the middle of a sandwich. She took off her shawl and kerchief and laid them on the back of the nearest overstuffed chair as she surveyed the parlor.

"Sit down, Rosie," Johnny said, "and I'll tell you about a wondrous piece of good luck I was able to send your way."

This place was nothing like their snug, cozy home in Ireland. Rose glanced around at the faded, dark-plush-upholstered furniture, the chipped tables, and the single framed print on the wall—a scene of the Irish shoreline north of Dublin—and said, "Can you let your good news wait a minute, while you show me where the stove is and I make us all a cup of tea?"

"You're hungry," Johnny said. "With all the excitement of greeting you, it never occurred to me that you'd be needing something to eat. All right, Rosie. I'll show you your room and the kitchen, and I'll wait until you're enjoying your tea before I tell you my news."

Rose's room was plain and neat with a double bed, a small chest of drawers, and a wardrobe for hanging clothes. On the chest was a note with her name on it. Recognizing her father's handwriting, she quickly tore it open.

*Dear Daughter Rose,* she read, *I'm sorry I wasn't at the train station to meet you. I have a good-paying job, and they're not that easy to come by, so I must work. I'm sending Johnny to get you and bring you home. I'll see you tonight.*

Underneath was his formal signature, *Peter John Carney.*

Rose smiled at the signature. Her father was not a man who found it easy to say what was in his heart, but he had left the note to show his love, and Rose treasured it.

She put the envelope on top of her suitcase, which Johnny had slung on the bed, and followed him down the hall to a room at the back. It was large enough to hold an upright ice chest and a worn round oak table and six chairs. There was a small sink under a window and close by a gleaming, ornate stove.

Johnny smiled proudly. "Won't Ma love that stove? It would have cost fifteen ninety-five if I'd bought it at Sears Roebuck, but I was able to get a terrific deal from one

16

of the city suppliers. Can you believe it? Brand new and only ten dollars!"

Would Ma love that stove? Rose was sure Ma would miss her big, solid black iron stove and would have to get used to this shining, overdecorated monstrosity, but Rose was not about to let a stove intimidate her. She pushed up her sleeves and picked up the handle for the four round lids. As she slid the handle into the slot on the nearest lid and lifted it, she spoke with surprise. "The stove's cold."

"There's no need to light the coal until you want to use it," Johnny said and reached for a few sheets of newspaper and a box of matches.

"Coal? What are you saying? Where's the peat?"

"In the United States they burn coal or wood, not peat." He removed one of the stove lids, wadded up the newspaper, and stuffed it inside. He scooped some lumps of coal from the bin next to the stove and placed them on top of the newspaper before he dropped in the lighted match. He watched and waited until the newspaper caught and the coals began to glow.

"Are you telling me there's no place around Chicago to dig blocks of peat and dry them?" Rose demanded.

"I'm telling you there's no peat at all."

"I thought this was a civilized country," Rose said, shaking her head. "I'm afraid there's much I'll have to get used to."

Johnny patted her shoulder. "You'll learn in no time. You're bright enough—for a girl."

Laughing, he ducked the slap she sent his way and stood in the doorway. "The kettle's on the stove, as you can see. There's a faucet for cold running water at the

17

sink, and the tin of tea is in the cupboard." He pointed at the ice chest. "You'll find cheese in there, along with a bit of sliced beef, and there's a half loaf of store-bought bread in the box on top." He gave a loud sigh and said, "It's going to be good to have real, home-baked bread again."

"You could have learned to bake it yourself!" Rose shouted after him, but Johnny had disappeared.

Rose managed to get the teakettle boiling and sand-wiches made. She found a dented tray with chips in its painted floral design, wiped it off with a damp cloth, and set the cups and saucers, pot, and sandwich plate on it.

Nowhere could she find napkins, and she worried what Tim Ryan would think. Well, never mind. She was not responsible for Tim Ryan, and the tea was getting cold. Rose carried the tray to the parlor and put it down on the nearest table. "Now," she said to her brother, "you can tell me the good news you've been holding in all this time."

Johnny munched through a large bite of his sandwich before he answered. "It's good news for *you*, Rosie. It's about your job. And you can thank me for it." He sat up a little straighter and looked important.

Rose had wondered if she'd have any trouble getting a job. She was eager to help save money for Ma's and the girls' passages and had hoped she'd get work as a servant for a well-off family, a common job with many single girls from Ireland, since they had no worries about room or board. "I do thank you, Johnny, for finding me a job so quickly," Rose said and put down her teacup. "Tell me. What is the family like? Are they good people?"

For a moment Johnny looked surprised, then his eyes

twinkled. "Household help, is it? You know, don't you, that the girls who take those jobs work up to eighteen hours a day, and their earnings come to only about four dollars a week?"

Rose took a deep breath before she answered, "Well, I'm sure to get a day off now and then to see my family, and if there's one thing I know how to do well it's keep a house clean, and . . ."

Johnny interrupted. "Rosie, Rosie, you're not going to be a servant. What I'm telling you is that because of the political connections I've made while working for Alderman Frank McMahan, I've been able to get you a really fine job as salesgirl in a dry-goods store owned by a man who owes a few favors to McMahan. You'll be paid seven dollars a week and have Sundays and evenings off. What could be better than that?"

"Not much, I'm thinking." Thankful that she wouldn't be spending her days scrubbing other people's floors, Rose grinned at Johnny. "But how will I know what to do and how to do it? And exactly what are these dry goods I'll be selling?"

"Bolts of material for ladies' dresses and coats, a few ready-made clothes, and some hats."

"Hats," Rose repeated as her elation disappeared. She glanced at her homespun kerchief and shawl draped over the top of the chair. "Johnny, I don't have a hat, and I'm sure I don't have the right clothes to work as a salesgirl."

"I hadn't thought about that part of it," Johnny said, "and I'm a little short of cash." He suddenly brightened. "Rosie, do you have any of your traveling money left?"

"A few cents over fifteen dollars."

Tim broke in. "Don't look so worried, Rose. That's

19

enough to get you most of the things you'll need. I'll ask my sister Kate to go shopping with you. She'll know where to find the best bargains."

"Thank you," Rose murmured and tried to smile, but she hated having to spend money on clothing when every single cent should go toward Ma's passage money.

Johnny tilted back his head and drained his cup of tea. "Let's go see Kate now," he said.

"Now?" Rose complained. "But I just got here. Truth be, I'm tired. I haven't even unpacked my things."

Johnny stood and held out a hand. "Tomorrow's Sunday, and Monday morning at seven o'clock sharp you report for work." He glanced toward the kitchen and sighed happily. "The store closes at six-thirty, so you'll be home by seven with plenty of time to cook dinner. The three of us—Da, Michael, and myself—aren't much for cooking, so you don't know how glad we are that we'll have a woman in the kitchen again."

Rose didn't answer. How often she'd heard her mother recite—usually with a smile—" 'Men work from rise to setting sun, but woman's work is never done.' " Well, that had always been the way of it, and she had more important things to think about. In spite of wanting to save every extra penny to bring the rest of her family to America, Rose couldn't help feeling just a little excited at the prospect of going shopping for new clothes.

Kate O'Malley, who was in her late twenties, already had crinkle lines around her eyes and mouth and a sprinkling of gray through her dark hair. She was friendly and kind, offering Rose a brown woolen coat she insisted she'd never be thin enough to wear again, and Rose liked her immediately. Kate left her two little boys in her mother-in-law's care, assured Tim and Johnny that she'd help Rose find her way home after the shopping trip, and took Rose on a cable car to the huge Sears, Roebuck and Company building between Jefferson and Desplaines streets.

Rose was overwhelmed by the tremendous number of items for sale. Her head swiveled from one side to the other as she surveyed cookware, baby buggies, carpenter's tools, men's shirts, and oak tables while Kate tugged her through the aisles.

"Shoes first," Kate said and made a sudden stop. "Boots like yours are not city wear, as I well know from having to make the change myself a few years ago."

Rose glanced at the array of stacked-heeled, pointed-toed, high-laced shoes and shuddered. "They'll pinch and hurt. I know they will."

"They do feel a little different, but you'll get used to them," Kate said. A clerk approached, and she told him, "My friend would like to see a nice pair of black leather shoes." She paused, glanced at Rose, and added, "Shoes that are as comfortable as possible."

"Certainly," he said. "Do you know the size?"

Kate looked at Rose, but Rose shook her head. The salesclerk gestured toward two empty chairs, and as soon as Kate and Rose were seated, he perched on a low stool in front of them and reached for Rose's right foot.

Rose pulled back in alarm. "What do you think you're up to?" she demanded.

"It's all right," Kate said. "He needs to take off your shoe so he can measure your foot."

"I can do it myself," Rose mumbled.

"This is part of his job," Kate told her. "Let him do it."

Rose allowed the clerk to remove her shoe, but her face burned with embarrassment and she couldn't meet his eyes.

He asked her to step on a board marked with numbers and lines, then stood and disappeared through a curtained doorway. Within a few moments the clerk returned with four boxes. He took a shoe from one of them and slipped it over Rose's stockinged foot.

"Ouch!" she said. "That's too tight."

"You'll be wearing a thinner stocking," he explained, and Rose blushed again, angry at herself for feeling ashamed of the thick woolen stockings her mother had knit for her.

"Nevertheless, I don't like the feel of the shoe," she said stubbornly.

"How much are those shoes?" Kate asked.

"Two ninety-five," the clerk answered.

Rose gasped, and the clerk looked indignant. "You won't find quality like that at a better price anywhere," he said. "Our store lives up to its motto: The Cheapest Supply House on Earth."

Kate leaned forward and asked the clerk, "Do you have anything a little less expensive?"

"As a matter of fact, I do," he replied. "I didn't realize that price was our main concern. We've got a style that's one of our most popular at only two dollars and fifteen cents. It's lined throughout with genuine kid, it has a cushion felt inner sole, and it laces up above the ankle."

"My friend would like to try them on," Kate said, with a firm look in Rose's direction.

Rose quietly submitted to having the first shoe removed and the second put on her foot. As soon as it was laced she stood. "It's snug," she said, "but it does feel better than the first."

"Try on the left shoe, too," the clerk said. "We want to make sure they are both a good fit. One foot is always bigger than the other, you know."

Rose had never heard such foolishness. Back home, when your feet grew larger you either inherited boots someone else had outgrown, or you went to the shoemaker's and bought the next size flat-heeled boot, wearing it in comfort until it wore out or your feet changed size again. There was none of this measuring and lacing and comparing one foot to another.

Dutifully, she tried on both shoes, walking across a short strip of carpet and back. "They feel very strange," she told Kate.

"Do they hurt or pinch anywhere?" Kate asked.

"I guess not."

"Then she'll take them," Kate told the clerk. With a sympathetic glance at Rose she said, "Please wrap them. For now she'll wear her boots."

Rose paid for the shoes and carried the wrapped package gingerly, glad that the shoes were still in the box and not on her feet. "Now should I buy a shirtwaist and skirt?" she asked Kate.

"You'll need the underpinnings first," Kate told her as she led the way across the store.

"What in the world are underpinnings?"

Kate drew Rose to the side of the aisle and looked at her intently. "It wasn't so many years ago that I was just like you, Rose. I was right off the boat, not knowing

23

anything but the farm I'd grown up on. I'd never seen fitted underskirts and corsets. I had no idea . . ."

"Corsets?" Rose interrupted. "Oh, I've seen corsets in the Dublin stores. They squeeze you in the middle and push everything up in front and out behind. Are you telling me I'll have to wear one of those things?"

"If you're a salesgirl in a fine dry-goods store you'll have to look fashionable," Kate said.

"What kind of a country is this United States?" Rose asked indignantly, but her eyes began to twinkle, and she grinned. "I'm paying good money that could be well spent elsewhere just so that I can feel uncomfortable from head to toe! I'm thinking I should be like your brother Tim and plan to go back to Ireland."

Kate shot Rose a startled, appraising glance, then took her arm and led her back into the aisle. "I hope," she said firmly, "you won't give serious thought to anything Tim happens to tell you."

# CHAPTER THREE

❖ ❖ ❖

R OSE unlocked the door of the Carney flat with the
key Johnny had given her and dropped her parcels
from Sears Roebuck on the nearest chair. The packages
of mutton chops and potatoes she kept in her arms.
"Kate," she said, "I'm pretty sure I remember how
Johnny lit the stove. Let me make you a cup of tea."

Kate smiled. "A few more minutes away from the children won't be amiss. I'd love a cup of tea." She followed
Rose to the kitchen, where Rose tucked the meat inside
the ice chest. Seeing that the tray under the steadily melt-
ing block of ice was full, she dumped the water into the
sink and replaced the empty tray.

"There are biscuits in the pantry," Rose said. "I found
a tin."

"Thank you, Rose. That reminds me," Kate murmured. "I
promised to bring some shortbread to Hull House tonight."

Rose saw to her satisfaction that the wadded newspaper had caught and the coals were beginning to burn. As she put the lid back on the stove she asked, "What's Hull House?"

"How can I describe it? It's a center over on Halsted Street, west and north from here, but it's a special place. Immigrants, neighbors, anyone who wants to come is welcome. At Hull House anyone can attend lectures, art exhibits, social programs, and there are even classes for children and for adults."

"Is it a school?"

"No, except for its kindergarten. It's more of a community center. Miss Jane Addams believes that just because people are poor doesn't mean that they aren't interested in learning. That's why she established Hull House in a neighborhood where people need help to improve their lot."

"So it's not exactly a school, and it's not just social. I'm sure there was nothing like it in Ireland."

Kate smiled. "You can find almost anything going on in Hull House. When I was there on Tuesday last, a baby was being cared for after its operation for a cleft palate. And Miss Addams was entertaining two professors from Denmark—or was it Sweden?—who had come for a meeting about world peace."

Rose dropped a scoop of tea leaves into the pot and filled it with the boiling water. "This place is run by a woman?"

"Jane Addams. She's a very special lady, and a very rich one, who founded Hull House. She lives right on the property." Kate accepted the cup Rose gave her and sat at the kitchen table. "Come with me some time, Rose," she said. "You'll like going. There are many times when my life needs a bit of cheering up, and Hull House provides that."

"I'm not a great one for lectures, but I only know you and my family. It would be nice to get out," Rose answered. She waited a moment, watching the steam curl up from her cup, then asked, "Do the men ever go?"

"If you mean our family men, no," Kate answered shortly. As she slowly stirred a dollop of milk into her tea, she added, "But Tim just might go, if *you* asked him to, Rose."

"Maybe I will—someday," Rose answered quietly.

"I hope you do. What Tim might learn at Hull House could do him some good." Kate gave a shake of her head as if to push away her worries.

As soon as Kate left, Rose put away her purchases. As she laid the corset in one of the dresser drawers, she shuddered. Imagine wasting thirty-nine cents on that monstrous garment of satin and netting, with its six long steel bars from top to bottom! Even worse, she'd have to wear it!

The hat was a different matter. "Proper and girlish," Kate had said approvingly of the black split-straw sailor. Rose approved of the hat, too. She liked the simple faille ribbon and bow better than the plumed and flowered hats for older women, and she liked the price—sixty-five cents.

The navy-blue skirt of heavy-duty melton kersey cloth that Rose had chosen was fitted around the hips, slightly flared at the bottom, and trimmed at the hem with double rows of black braid; and there was a jacket to match. Her two shirtwaists, which buttoned up the front with a minimum of tucks at each side, were of white cotton with high, tight collars and wrist-length sleeves, puffed at the top. Kate had told her the sleeves were called leg-of-mutton. Strange name. Strange country.

Rose sighed, feeling that when she put on all those trappings she'd turn into someone she didn't know. Oh, how terribly she missed her mother and her home in Ireland where she could bundle in her shawl in the winter or run barefoot through the soft grass in the summer—where she could be just plain Rose Carney. But now she didn't know what she'd become. It was so hard to realize she'd only arrived in Chicago that morning.

She wondered how soon Tim was going back to Ireland and how he could afford to. Maybe one of these days he'd tell her. If not, she might just ask. She smiled to herself as she realized that question was only one of many she had about Tim Ryan.

It was close to seven o'clock by the time Rose had tidied the house, lit the oil lamps, and prepared potatoes both to roast in the oven and simmer on the stove. She had browned the mutton chops with a bit of onion, and they slowly cooked in a covered iron skillet. Now and then she held the front curtains aside and peered into the darkness, watching nervously for her father to arrive.

Should she run to him with a hug, as she had when she was a little girl, or would he expect her to behave with dignity like a grown woman? Why, oh, why couldn't she remember his face?

As she heard footsteps on the stairs, Rose dropped the spoon she was holding and ran toward the parlor.

The door opened. Johnny glanced around the room,

then flung his derby hat at the top of a coat tree near the door, where it wobbled, then hung.

"Looks like I'm the first one home," he said. He walked toward the hallway to the bedrooms, tugging off his suit coat, cravat, and stiff linen collar; but he paused, closed his eyes, and took a deep, exaggerated breath. "Ahhh! Something smells wonderful, Rosie."

Michael, dressed in workman's clothes, arrived just moments after Johnny and swept Rose off her feet in a gigantic hug while he, too, sniffed the air appreciatively. "Already it smells like the house did in the old days," he said and set Rose down with a thump.

"If you'll remember, we didn't have mutton chops—or any kind of meat—that often," Rose told him. She put her hands on her hips and tried to look stern. "And what's all this concern about what's going into your stomach? Where's the 'Did you have a good trip, Rose?' or 'How are Ma and the little girls, Rose?'"

Her brother Michael still looked like a picture of a large, friendly bear Rose had seen in one of her schoolbooks. He pulled off his billed workman's cap and said contritely, "I'm sorry, Rosie. You just don't know what the meals have been like around here." He gave her a tentative smile. "How *was* your trip? Better than mine was, I hope, with the hold crowded and stinking of vomit, and the food not fit to feed pigs."

"Enough of that," Johnny interrupted as he returned to the parlor. "Traveling steerage to America is nothing we want to remember. A simple 'Glad to see you, Rosie' would have been enough."

Rose heard other, slower footsteps on the stairs. Her palms were wet, and she found it hard to breathe. "Why don't you both wash up?" she said quickly with a glance at Michael's dirty overalls. "We'll eat as soon as Da gets home."

"He doesn't always . . ." Michael began, but Johnny interrupted him again.

"Rosie said to wash up, so let's be at it," he ordered, and the two men walked through the parlor toward the kitchen, where towels were hung next to the sink.

As the doorknob rattled, Rosie hurried toward it. She grasped the knob and swung the door inward. Her father, still bent with his key in hand, looked up in surprise. His mouth dropped open and he gasped. "Maura!"

"No, Da. It's me . . . Rosie."

Peter Carney straightened, and Rose smiled. His dear, familiar face. How could she have forgotten it? There were wrinkles around his eyes, and the skin drooped around his chin and jowls, but the hair that escaped from under his cap was still thick and black.

His eyes brightened with recognition and he beamed. "Rosie! You're the image of your mother many years ago! For a moment I thought . . ."

"Oh, Da," Rose murmured and ran into his arms.

Tenderly he held her, his tears wetting her own cheek.

"Don't cry, Da," Rose whispered. "You know Johnny found me a job, and I'll work hard. We'll be able to bring Ma and the girls over in no time at all."

Her father released her and mopped at his face with a large cotton handkerchief, stained—as were his hands, his overalls, and his denim jacket—with brick and mortar dust. "In no time at all," he repeated. "That's right, Rosie."

Rose could smell the whiskey on her father's breath. It

30

puzzled her. Aside from a nip or two on special holidays, Da had never been a drinking man. *Da was probably as nervous about seeing me again as I was about seeing him,* Rose told herself, and put it out of her mind.

With a contrite smile he reached over and wiped her cheek with his handkerchief, showing her a smudge of black.

Rose clapped a hand to the spot he had rubbed.

"It's not you, Rosie girl. It's the boot black I put around the temples each day to cover the gray. Because work on some of the taller buildings is dangerous, the contractors don't like to give jobs to the older men."

Rose felt a sudden jolt of fear. "If the work's dangerous, then maybe you shouldn't be doing it."

His voice took on a teasing tone as he said, "Everything in life has its dangers. Crossing a street with a trolley coming could be dangerous. Leaning out an open window to talk to a neighbor could be dangerous. Don't fret yourself about it, Rosie. Promise me you won't."

"All right, Da," she answered.

During supper the men ate with such eager concentration that Rose did all the talking. She told them about her shopping trip with Kate. "Our last stop was at the Maxwell Street market, out of doors. All those carts and vendors! I've never seen such food! It looked like enough to feed all of Ireland!"

Johnny laughed. "It's not enough to feed even a portion of Chicago. You'll find other markets like that which are just as busy."

Rose reached into her pocket, pulled out a small handful of pennies, and placed them on the table. "After having to buy work clothes and a few things that were

31

needed in the larder, this is all I have left of my traveling money—seven cents. Where do you keep the money you're saving for Ma's passage?"

Michael spoke up. "We take a portion from each of our paychecks—whatever we can spare after putting aside money for our living expenses and for Ma's—and put it into a quart canning jar at the back of the pantry."

"It's not a set amount?"

"Sometimes we have more to spare than other times," Johnny explained. "Occasionally, there's a need to spend money for a new pair of shoes or a bit of socializing. I heard that Michael's courting a girl, although he hasn't told us about her yet."

A dark red swept over Michael's face. "There's been no need to say anything about her. She's a fine young woman, and she understands that there will be no ring and no nuptial Mass at the church until all the family's been brought over. A walk in the park on Sunday is not costly."

Rose reached across the table and covered Michael's hand with her own. Smiling, she said, "I'd like to meet her, Michael. What's her name?"

His voice was so low Rose could hardly hear the words. "Ellen Derry," he mumbled.

Da nodded with satisfaction. "A good Irish girl then," he said. "Catholic, as well?"

"Yes," Michael said. "And she's kind and beautiful and wonderful."

"Why haven't we met this kind, beautiful, wonderful girl?" Johnny teased.

Michael stood. His ears no longer looked as though they were on fire, but his voice was deep and tight as he

32

scowled at his brother. "There will be no more talk about Ellen, not until we are ready to make arrangements for our wedding." He gulped painfully. "And because of the circumstances, that will not be for at least two years."

Eager to change the subject for Michael's sake, Rose asked, "Where in the pantry do you keep the jar of money?"

Michael strode to the pantry, stretched to reach behind the parcels and containers of food, and pulled out a fat glass canning jar. A few bills and a small pile of coins lay in the bottom of the jar.

As he placed it on the table he examined it. "I thought there was more in the jar than this."

"We took what we needed for Rosie's passage, her train travel, and the twenty-five dollars she needed to enter the United States," Da said.

Michael frowned. "I know, but after we bought Rosie's passage we began contributing again."

Johnny held out his hands and smiled. "Don't look at me. I didn't help myself to any of that. I even put in an extra dollar."

"Wait a minute," Rosie said. "Don't you keep a record of what goes in here?"

"No," Michael answered. "We just put in what we can."

"Then no wonder there's so much confusion." Rose swept her hands down over her apron in a smoothing motion—realizing with a pang that it was a decisive gesture she'd often seen her mother make—and said, "I'll put a piece of paper and a pencil in the pantry, along with the jar. Before the next weekly paychecks, we'll have a talk and decide what each of us can contribute. Then, as we add it we'll write it down."

"Now, Rosie," her father said good-naturedly. "You just arrived here and aren't used to our ways as yet. We have a system, and it worked to get you and your brothers here."

Johnny grinned. "That's the way of all women," he said. "Always wanting to take charge. Just wait until Michael and Ellen . . ."

As Michael took a quick step toward him, Johnny jumped from his chair to place the table between them. "I remember, no more talk about the kind, beautiful, and wonderful Ellen Derry." He made a dash from the room.

Rose looked up at Michael, expecting to see an angry frown, but Michael was smiling. "Ellen *is* kind and beautiful and wonderful," he said.

As Da got to his feet Michael clapped a hand on his shoulder. "I think Rosie is right about deciding on the amount of contributions and keeping a record," he said. "The sooner we get Ma and the girls here, the better it will be for all of us.

Again he blushed, and Rose laughed.

"We'll see, we'll see," her father said as he walked from the room, Michael following.

Rose surveyed the stacks of dirty dishes and pans and rolled up her sleeves, eager to finish the job. She was exhausted.

Tomorrow would be Sunday, and Rose was grateful for that one day during which she could catch her breath and prepare to begin a job for which—as far as she knew—she'd be totally unsuited.

# CHAPTER FOUR

❖ ❖ ❖

THE next morning Rose ignored her new clothes, even though her father and brothers wore dark suits and derby hats, and wore her homespun dress, shawl, and kerchief to Sunday Mass. Along the long walk to St. Columbanus many of the women Rose saw were also dressed in the clothes from their mother countries.

Although the Carneys arrived ten minutes before Mass was to begin, the church was nearly filled. Rose knelt to say a prayer before the tabernacle, then climbed over Michael into the aisle and made her way to the statue of Mary, the mother of Jesus. The statue, with welcoming arms outstretched to each side, was banked with flowers, and candlelight flickered in the small red glass votive cups in the stand directly behind the padded kneeler.

Rose knelt, made the Sign of the Cross, and gazed up at the statue, so much like the one in the convent in

Drogheda that she allowed the warm familiarity to soothe away much of the trepidation she felt about what was expected of her in this new country.

The bells in the church tower began to ring, signifying that Mass was soon to begin, so Rose quickly got to her feet. She returned to the pew as the priest and altar boys entered the sanctuary and began the opening prayers of the Mass at the foot of the altar. Rose was familiar with the prayers said in Latin—thanks primarily to Sister Rita—and mentally recited the Confiteor, the Kyrie, and the Gloria along with the priest.

But after the readings of the Epistle and Gospel, while the tall, elderly priest—with a brogue straight from home—delivered his sermon, Rose's mind began to wander. She couldn't keep from thinking about the job she would begin the following day. Would the shop owner be understanding if she didn't learn quickly? What if she made mistakes in giving change while getting used to the currency of this country? And how could she possibly survive an entire day inside that waist-squeezing metal-boned corset?

Rose gave a start of surprise as those around her suddenly stood for the Creed. The sermon was over, and for the life of her Rose couldn't remember what Father had been talking about. During the rest of the Mass she tried her best to concentrate on her prayers, but there was so much on her mind it was hard to do.

After Mass Rose met their upstairs neighbors, Mr. and Mrs. O'Brien. They were only three months here from Ireland, and Mrs. O'Brien, about the age of Kate, was obviously in a family way.

The Horbowys were sitting on the steps of the house,

enjoying the sunshine, when the Carneys returned. They were an older couple with two nearly grown boys, and their English was understandable, for the most part. They asked Rose about her journey and related the horrors of their own trip across the ocean.

For the Carneys' main meal there was a large pot of soup, which Rose had put on the stove to simmer before they left for Mass, and freshly baked soda bread, which disappeared all of five minutes after Da had said the grace before the meal. Feeding her father and two brothers was going to be a demanding job.

Da patted his full stomach and said, "I think I'll take a little walk down to Casey's."

"Who is Casey?" Rose asked. "One of the neighbors?"

"Casey's is a pub," Michael said, and he frowned as he glanced at their father.

"Call it what you will, it's nothing more than a comfortable place for friends to get together," Da said and smiled, ignoring the look Michael was giving him. "It's where some of the boys go to relax and talk over old times."

Rose thought about her Sunday noon meals at home when she was a child and they were all together. Sometimes they had enough to eat, sometimes the meals were meager, but in any case her father would always pat his stomach and say, "There never was a cook as good as Maura Carney." Then he'd pull on his jacket and go outside to tend to the animals.

Later, Rose would often see him leaning on the rock wall that separated the Carneys' small plot of farm from their neighbor's. Her father and a neighbor or two would be deep in conversation, "solving the problems of the world," as her father liked to put it.

But here they were surrounded by crowded houses, cramped together block after block. It must not be easy for neighbors to find a relaxing spot where they could talk to one another. Rose realized that her father missed those visits with friends.

"Da," Michael said, "why don't you take Rosie to Jackson Park? She hasn't seen some of the good-looking parts of Chicago."

Johnny pushed back his chair and stood. "That's a fine idea, Da. I'd like to go with you, but I'm meeting with the Clan na Gaelers."

"The Clan na Gaelers?" Rose cried. "They were the ones responsible for the bombings in England!"

"Don't fret about the past, Rosie," Michael answered. "The Clan na Gael has new leaders, and there's been no talk of violence."

"Not with the Clan na Gael itself," Da broke in with a wink. "But I have my doubts about that splinter group Johnny meets with. How about it, Johnny? What do those lads have up their sleeves?"

"Something for the good of Ireland," Johnny said. "That's all I'll tell you."

"Johnny!" Rose cried, fearful of what Johnny was hiding. "You know what Ma has always said about working out our problems with peaceful discussions."

"So far peaceful discussions have led nowhere."

"It takes time."

Johnny's easy manner disappeared. Angrily he asked, "What is it going to take to rightfully return our country to the Irish? The injustice of it all is why so many of us had to leave Ireland and come here."

"I don't have an easy answer for you," Rose said. "But hotheaded actions without any thought behind them don't solve anything."

"Sitting around waiting like a bump on a log for something to happen doesn't solve anything either," Johnny snapped.

Da sighed. "It's hard to forget the great famine with starving people dying in roadside ditches while British gentry rode past unheeding and uncaring."

"Don't encourage him, Da!" Rose warned.

For an instant Johnny's eyes darkened, but Rose saw composure slip over him like a cloak, and when he smiled he was the same teasing, mischief-loving brother she knew. Jauntily, he strode from the kitchen, Michael and Da following.

Rose filled the teakettle and set it on the stove to heat water for washing the dishes. The sooner she finished cleaning up, the sooner she and her father could leave for the park. Michael had been right about one thing. She would love seeing something more of Chicago than crowded, soot-stained buildings.

"Rosie girl."

She turned to see that her father was already dressed for outside in his suit coat and derby. "Oh, Da, I won't be ready for a little while, but I'll hurry," Rose said.

"Take your time," he answered. "I'll just run down to Casey's for a few moments with the boys while you're putting the kitchen in order."

"It won't take much time. Just fifteen or twenty minutes."

"I'll be back by then," he insisted, and before she could say another word he had left the room.

There was nothing else to do but take him at his word, so Rose scraped plates, washed them in the hot suds, and scrubbed the table.

By the time she finished, her father hadn't returned, so she peeled potatoes for the evening meal, covering them with water and setting the pot on the back of the stove. She washed and chopped a head of cabbage, also covering it with water. If they lingered at the park until it was late, then there would be little left to do for the meal than light the stove and fry a pound of bacon to go with the vegetables.

Rose walked to the front window to look out at the street. Where was Da? How much longer would he be?

Michael came into the room, stopped when he saw Rose, and shook his head. "I'm afraid that Da won't be home for a good long while," he told her.

"He promised he would."

"He doesn't remember his promises when he's drinking."

"When did he start with the drinking?" Rose took a deep breath and steadied herself for Michael's answer.

"He's lonely, Rosie. He misses Ma something terrible."

"That's no reason to . . ."

"He's a farmer, good at working the land, but there are no farm jobs available here, so he works as an unskilled laborer in a job he hates. He tries to make the best of it, but the whole thing is too much for him. His only consolation is meeting with his friends who are all in the same boat. They talk about the old days, and maybe they make them seem a little better than they were."

Rose was shocked. "Are you saying it's all right?"

Michael shook his head. "No. We agree it's not all right. I'm saying we have to understand his problem. Then it will be easier to help him."

"Whiskey costs money. That money could be better spent toward Ma's and the little girls' passage." Rose thought about the money in the canning jar, shivering as she asked, "It was Da who helped himself to money from the jar, wasn't it?"

"Don't be hard on him, Rosie," Michael said. "He's working as hard as he can to bring Ma here."

"I've a lot to think about," she answered, "and much of it hurts. I just wish Ma was here to make things right."

Michael rested a hand on Rose's shoulder and smiled. "It's a fine spring day with the sun bright and warm, not a day for staying indoors. Come with me. Ellen and I will take you to Jackson Park." His voice dropped shyly as he said, "I'd like you and Ellen to meet each other."

Rose took a step backward. "Not now. I'm still upset. Ellen and I should meet when . . ."

"You and Ellen should meet *now*," Michael said firmly. "Wash your face. You're going to enjoy a day in the park."

"How should I dress? What will Ellen be wearing?"

"What difference does it make? The dress you have on is fine. Hurry, Rosie! Now! We don't want to keep Ellen waiting."

Dutifully, Rose scrubbed her face and brushed her hair before tying on her kerchief and swinging her shawl over her shoulders. She tried to push her father's problem out of her mind, but she was still badly shaken by the news. Attempting to help, Michael kept up a steady one-sided conversation as they walked the long blocks to the house where Ellen lived.

Rose couldn't help noticing that the neighborhood was changing for the better. Houses were larger and set farther apart on their lots. Many of the homes had been built of brick or stone and had rounded tower rooms, cupolas, and sheltered wraparound porches. There were lawn swings and large trees with widespread branches and women sitting on the porches in soft white dresses.

"Michael!" Rose whispered. "You didn't tell us that Ellen is rich!"

Michael chuckled before he answered. "Ellen isn't rich. She works as a lady's maid." He took Rose's elbow and steered her around a corner and through a walkway that led to the back door of an immense, yellow stone house.

He lifted a hand to knock, but the door quickly opened, and a short, blond woman stepped outside. She gave a quick smile to Rose, but she beamed at Michael. She wore a forest-green skirt and fitted jacket that emphasized her tiny waist—"*Corsets,*" Rose muttered to herself—and on her head was a fashionable hat decorated with gray and black plumes that curled under her chin.

"Ellen, this is my sister Rosie," Michael said. He took Ellen's hand and led her toward Rose. "I've told her all about you, and she's been eager to meet you. She'll be spending the day with us."

"You *are* beautiful, just as Michael said," Rose blurted out. Feeling large and clumsy and awkward, she fervently wished she'd worn her new clothes, wished she'd stayed home where she belonged, wished that she'd never come to America in the first place.

"It's all thanks to my mistress, who is generous with

42

her cast-off clothing," Ellen said and winked as though Rose were an old friend sharing a good joke.

*I like her already,* Rose thought, *and I'm going to like having a sister close to my own age.* The world immediately became a happier place.

# CHAPTER FIVE

❖ ❖ ❖

JACKSON Park was larger and more impressive than Rose had imagined. Following the shore of the great Lake Michigan, the park's wide lawns and trees spread out like green paint from a spilled bucket. A large, round bed had been dug and planted with small, already-blooming seedlings of orange-and-yellow marigolds.

Rose stopped, inhaling the damp pungency of the freshly dug earth, and remembered with a pang the newly turned clods of dark, broken soil at corn-planting time. During this season Da wore this same deep, earthy fragrance on his clothing, his hair, and even in the sweat on the back of his neck.

They passed a small lake on which people boated and fished, and Ellen tugged playfully at Michael's arm. "Let's rent a boat. It's such a lovely day for being on the water."

Michael looked embarrassed. "I don't have enough

money with me, Ellen. There's barely enough to cover carfare home."

Ellen's smile didn't waver. "Well, for that matter," she said, "a walk along the shore is really what I've been dreaming of all week, and we couldn't have a nicer day for it, could we?"

As she crooked an arm through Rose's, Ellen said, "Michael told me about your fine new job as salesgirl. I'm happy for you."

Rose glanced down at her old-country clothing. "I—I won't dress like this. I've already bought a shirtwaist and skirt and . . . and the other things I'll need."

"You'll look fine," Ellen said. She turned and stood on tiptoe, pulling off Rose's kerchief with one hand and twisting a strand of hair upward. "You have beautiful hair. Sweep it up like this. Do you have hairpins?"

"Yes," Rose said.

"I had to learn so much when I came. The lady of the house was very patient with me and taught me how to look and behave."

"How to behave? What do you mean?"

"Well, there are certain little things that employers like. I must walk softly and dip a small curtsey when spoken to and keep my aprons freshly starched and ironed and . . ." Ellen's voice dropped to a whisper and she made a face as she added, "And always wear a corset."

Together Rose and Ellen burst into laughter, and Michael asked, "What's so funny? Can you share the joke?"

"No!" Ellen said, and the girls laughed again.

As they resumed their stroll Rose asked, "Do you like the family you're working for? Are they good people?"

"They're as good as any," Ellen said, "maybe better than some. The working hours are long—six in the morning until ten at night—but they don't stint on food for the staff, or heat for the bedrooms. John, the butler, is a sour apple if there ever was one, but our cook, Berta, knows how to keep him in line." Before Rose could ask another question, Ellen said, "It's hard work, but I don't mind it. Cleaning house is what I was doing back in Ireland, and it's what I'll be doing after Michael and I are married. It's something I know how to do and do well."

"Which is more than I can say about the job I'll be starting tomorrow," Rose murmured.

Ellen squeezed her arm. "Don't worry," she said. "Nothing is going to go wrong, and you'll learn what you need to do in a hurry." She turned toward Michael. "Berta's daughter is going to marry that policeman who's been taking her out. You should hear what Berta has to say about a policeman's job."

"It would be dangerous, wouldn't it?" Rose broke in.

"No more dangerous than working high up on a building under construction, as Michael does."

"You've said before that I should apply for a job on the force," Michael told her, "but I wouldn't know the first thing about being a police officer."

"They'd teach you."

"I don't even know what qualifications they ask for."

Ellen's cheeks grew pink. "Well, I do," she said. "I asked Berta to find out. All you need is to be a young man in good health—which you *are*, Michael!" She bounced on her toes as she said, "And I found out what policemen are paid! You'll never believe this, Michael—

47

up to five dollars a day! That's much better than what you're getting as a day laborer—a dollar seventy-five a day."

Michael stopped in surprise. "The beginning salary is bound to be lower," he said.

"Not that much lower."

"I'll think about it," he answered. Rose hoped Ellen knew Michael's thinking about it would take awhile. Michael was a deliberate kind of person, turning an idea around and around in his mind the way he'd examine an apple for bruised spots.

Rose let the two of them talk while she gazed out at the lake—as large as an ocean—and allowed the serenity of the glistening water to fill her mind.

She was surprised when she heard Michael say, "Rosie, it's time to turn back."

"There'll be a next time," Ellen said. "We'll all come here again soon."

Rose smiled at the two of them, glad that Ellen was going to become her sister. "You were right, Michael," she said. "This trip to the park was just what I needed. The world seems right again."

That evening, before she cooked supper, Rose counted the money in the canning jar and wrote the amount with the date on a sheet of paper. Then she hid the jar among the potatoes in the large burlap potato sack. No one would be likely to look for it there.

Michael came into the kitchen as Rose was carving thick slices from the slab of bacon. "Da's home," he said.

Rose laid down the knife and looked up, relieved. "Is he . . . all right?"

"Of course he is," Michael said. He looked away, then back at Rose. "Go easy on him, Rosie. You had your trip to Jackson Park, and you met Ellen, and the three of us had a fine time, didn't we?"

"Yes," Rose said and tried to smile, but she ached inside, missing her mother so terribly she could hardly bear it. "When Ma gets here," she said, "Da will be his old self again, won't he?"

"I'm sure he will," Michael said, and brightened, obviously glad to change the subject. "I haven't had a chance to ask you, Rosie. What do you think of my Ellen?"

"She's everything you said she was and more. I'm honestly glad the two of you will be getting married," Rose answered.

"Thank you, Rosie." Michael wrapped her in a bear hug.

"Don't thank me. It's you who had the good luck to find her." Rose pulled herself free and made a shooing motion. "Now get out of my kitchen, Michael, so I can get supper ready."

The meal went much better than Rose had expected. Da was lavish with praise for her cooking, comparing her skills with her mother's.

"How was your day in Jackson Park, Rosie?" he asked. "I should have come, but the time got away from me. I hope you understand."

"Of course I do," Rosie said, trying to ease his embarrassment. "It's a beautiful park with the lake and all that green grass and . . . Oh, Da, there were fresh-turned flower beds with marigolds newly planted. Just the smell of that earth reminded me of our farm."

Da rested his fork on the edge of his plate and studied

49

her a moment. "There were gardeners at work in the park?"

"It's Sunday," she said. "There wasn't a gardener in sight."

"They'd need plenty, no fear, for the size of the parks in this city," Da said and went back to his meal.

Michael began telling a humorous story, and Johnny tried to top him. It wasn't until Rose stood to scrape and wash the dishes that her father put an arm around her shoulders and quietly said, "Rosie, the time just got away from me today, but I've got something in mind for you— something I've been planning for some time."

"That's fine, Da," Rose said and reached for a plate.

"You say it's fine, but you don't know what it is," he teased. "It's better than fine." He gripped her shoulders and turned her so that she looked into his face. "I'm talking about your birthday, Rosie girl. In three weeks— June seventh. We'll do something to make it special. Did you think your father would forget such an important day?"

Rose was touched, but she was embarrassed. "I'll be sixteen, Da—a woman. Birthday celebrations are for children."

When she was a child, Rose loved to remember, Ma would make a pudding and put a sprig of wildflowers on the table. Sometimes there'd be a special treat like sugar-candy drops. Once Ma had given her a rag doll with eyes, nose, and a mouth stitched from scraps of yarn.

Da's face sagged with concern. "You've got tears in your eyes, Rosie girl. What did I say to make you so sad?"

Rose threw her arms around her father and buried her

face against his shoulder. "It's Ma. I miss her so terribly much!"

"I miss your mother, too," Da said in a tone so woeful that Rose clung to her father even more tightly. There was nothing else to say.

In the morning Rose woke to the ringing of the alarm clock in her father's room. She pulled a wrapper over her nightgown, stoked and lit the stove, then set a filled teakettle over one of the lids. The darkness of night had faded to a dull gray by the time Rose had fried the eggs, sliced bread—she would have to make a fresh batch tonight—and made a pot of tea so dark and strong it would flip sleepy eyelids wide open.

Rose felt comfortable doing the tasks that Ma had always done so well. Someday she'd be even more like Ma, with her own husband and children to care for. She smiled at the thought, but there was too much to be done to daydream.

As soon as Rose had made and packed lunches for all of them she ate quickly, standing at the stove. One by one her brothers and father came to the table. She served them, then hurried to her room to dress. She wasn't eager to push and pull herself into that terrible corset and the tight-waisted skirt, but she did what had to be done.

It was not until she had swept up her hair the way Ellen had showed her and had fastened her hat on her head that Rose dared to look into the mirror.

"I knew it! It's not Rose Carney staring back at me. It's someone entirely different!" she said aloud.

There was a sharp knock at her door. "Talking to yourself, are you?" Johnny called. "Get a move on, Rosie.

I'll take you to Sweeney's this first day, and we'll have to leave no later than ten minutes from now."

"I'm hurrying," Rose called back. When she opened her door Johnny had gone back to his room, so she went to the kitchen to put the dishes to soak, careful not to soil her new clothes. There was no time to wash the breakfast things. She'd have to do the cleaning up tonight. How did other women manage to get everything done? Maybe she should take the alarm clock into her own room and get up fifteen minutes ahead of the others.

As Rose strode into the parlor, her father and brothers were at the door ready to leave. The three of them stared at her with wide eyes.

Johnny recovered first and exclaimed, "Rosie! You look like a model in an ad for Marshall Field's! You're a beauty!"

"Nonsense. I'm the same Rose Carney I was yesterday and the day before," Rose replied, but she glanced away, knowing she hadn't spoken the truth. She had left girlhood behind with her old clothes and had become a woman—the woman she'd seen in the mirror.

Johnny grinned. "My chum Tim Ryan thought you were pretty when he first saw you. He should see you now."

"Who cares what Tim Ryan thinks?" Rose said, but quickly looked away as she felt herself blushing.

"Tim Ryan?" Da asked.

"He's a friend of mine," Johnny said, and he flung open the front door. "Let's go, let's go! We don't want our Rosie to be late for work her very first day."

By trolley Sweeney's Dry Goods Store, on State Street, was a half hour's ride. Rose trembled as they arrived,

52

and the only thing that kept her from clinging to her brother was the cheerful appearance of Sweeney's store. Bright-green awnings were rolled down to shield pedestrians from the sun and protect the colorful bolts of material in the window display from fading.

The inside of the store was immediately intriguing to Rose. On one side were tables covered with huge bolts of fabric, and behind them was a wall covered with racks of buttons and colored braids, spools of thread and shiny silver thimbles, paper packs of pins and needles and bright red pincushions. There were scissors of all sizes and yellow-and-black tape measures.

On the other side of the store stood racks of ready-made clothes for women and children and shelves displaying hats for every occasion.

Mr. George Sweeney was short and stout with a pug-nosed face mapped by crinkle lines. He looked Rose over, nodded, and said, "You look like a proper young saleswoman, but I was told you've had no experience in the selling line."

"I learn quickly," Rose answered.

A smile twitched at his lips. "I also heard you were straight off the farm."

"I've had convent schooling," Rose said. "I'm good with sums."

Mr. Sweeney's smile deepened. "Welcome, Rose Carney. We'll see what you can do."

He turned to glance over his shoulder and called, "Catherine! Where are you?"

From behind a curtain at the back of the store a pudgy woman appeared. Wisps of gray hair had pulled out of the bun at the top of her head, and her apron was askew.

"I was shelving the stock," Catherine Sweeney said. "I suppose I look a sight." She straightened her apron and smiled at Rose. "You must be Rose Carney. We're glad to have you here. There's lots of work to do. We recently lost our full-time clerk and our part-time clerk. Both girls left to get married."

Rose began to feel a little less nervous. She liked the Sweeneys and decided she was going to like working for them.

She'd been asked to arrive before the store officially opened so Mrs. Sweeney could show Rose what to do. She was told where to hang her jacket and hat, where to store her handbag and lunch, how to fill out a sales slip, how to divide the bills and change in the cash register, and how to understand the American way of sizing clothes. "Don't worry, Rose," Mrs. Sweeney said. "If you have any questions, just call on me. I'll help you out."

As Mr. Sweeney turned the cardboard sign in the window from CLOSED to OPEN, a woman who had been studying the window display entered the store.

Rose walked over to the racks of clothes and took a deep breath, trying to steady herself as the customer approached, but the woman turned left into the fabric section of the store, and Rose relaxed with a sigh.

"Miss? Will you please help me?"

Rose turned to face a fashionably dressed young woman holding an equally fashionable toddler by the hand. The little girl was bundled in dark stockings and high buttoned shoes. Her many petticoats held out a ruffled cranberry-red skirt and a wide, ruffled, lace collar decorated a short, fitted jacket of the same shade. Lace

54

framed a bonnet through which a tiny face peered solemnly at Rose.

Rose's heart went out to the child, and she flashed her a smile. Someday she hoped to have a little girl as dear as this one.

"I'm sorry," Rose began to explain. "I didn't see you come in. How may I help you?"

"I'd like some summer dresses for my daughter. What do you have in white lawn?"

Rose quickly found what the woman was looking for, and the woman made her purchase. Rose filled out the sales slip without any trouble. She'd been nervous about handling the unfamiliar currency, but she deposited the dollars in the cash register, which gave a loud, satisfied ring as it opened.

The woman and her daughter who stood waiting were expecting something. Rose stared at the little dresses and wondered what she was supposed to do with them. How was she to wrap them up so as not to ruin them?

Suddenly Mrs. Sweeney appeared at Rose's side and began folding the dresses. "I'll lend you a hand in wrapping this parcel," she said, and as she did she chatted with the customer. First she talked about the weather and then discussed a new dessert called Jell-O that was making such a hit.

*A dessert you could see through? A dessert that shook and wiggled?* Rose was aware that her thoughts of Jell-O should be pushed aside. She had to concentrate on what Mrs. Sweeney was doing.

Mrs. Sweeney was a wonderful businessperson. She had the knack of talking easily to customers. Rose realized this was part of what she had to learn.

As soon as the customer left Rose began, "I'm sorry, Mrs. Sweeney. I should have known what to do. I guess I'm still nervous."

"It's not your fault," Mrs. Sweeney told her. "I didn't explain how to wrap the packages. Look—here's a roll of paper and here's the string. You saw what I did." She took a shirtwaist that was hanging nearby and placed it on the counter. "Remember, lay the garments facedown, then fold in each side toward the back, making sure the sleeves are flat, without wrinkles. Then fold here . . . and here . . . You can do it, Rose."

"Of course I can," Rose answered as she copied what Mrs. Sweeney had done.

The door opened and customers entered the store. Three women headed for the fabric section, where they were greeted by both Mr. and Mrs. Sweeney, but a middle-aged woman, even rounder and plumper than Mrs. Sweeney, bustled over to the ready-to-wear section.

Rose hurried over to her and asked, "May I help you?"

"Yes, thank you," the customer answered. "I'm looking for a silk waist. Black, I think. Maybe with ruffles around the yoke."

"I'm not that familiar with the merchandise yet," Rose said cheerfully, "but the waists are over against the wall. Let's take a look." She remembered what she had learned about sizes. "What size will you want? Thirty-eight? Forty?"

The woman bristled. "Thirty-four."

"Oh, it's for your daughter then. I didn't think the added bulk of ruffles would be something you'd want for yourself."

"Perhaps someone else could wait on me," the woman

said angrily and loudly, and Rose saw Mrs. Sweeney stop what she was doing and hurry toward them.

"Is there a problem?" she asked quietly.

"This young woman has been quite insulting," the customer snapped. "Asking me if my size is a thirty-eight or forty! And then telling me I don't want a waist with ruffles when that's exactly what I *do* want!"

"Rose," Mrs. Sweeney said, "suppose you unpack the boxes of merchandise in the storeroom. I'll be delighted to help Mrs. . . ?"

"Mrs. Horace Elverson," the woman replied firmly. "And I'd like a black silk waist with *ruffles*."

Her face burning with embarrassment, Rose hurried into the storeroom, where she immediately busied herself with the unpacking of boxes. She'd been at her job only a short while and already she'd made a customer unhappy. Most probably she'd be looking for another job tomorrow.

# CHAPTER SIX

✧ ✧ ✧

ROSE had finished the shelving of the contents of both large boxes by the time Mrs. Sweeney pulled back the curtain and entered the storeroom.

"I'm sorry for the terrible mistakes," Rose began. "If you'll give me another chance I'll . . ."

"That's enough, Rose," Mrs. Sweeney interrupted.

Rose took a deep breath and tried not to feel weak. Oh, how she wished her mother were here. "Will you want me to finish out the day?" she asked quietly.

"Is that what you've been thinking—that you're going to be dismissed?" Mrs. Sweeney slowly shook her head. "There's much to learn about being a good salesclerk, and it isn't picked up in one morning, let alone one day. There's only one customer in the store at the moment, and George is taking care of her, so now let me give you a little lesson about what went wrong. Keep in mind that you always give a customer what she wants."

"Even if she wants the wrong size? That woman could never get into a thirty-four waist."

"Yes, she could, if it were expensive enough, and we do carry a few expensive lines. The manufacturers of expensive clothes size them differently in order to flatter their customers. Mrs. Elverson is willing to pay extra, not just for quality but to convince herself she is still a size thirty-four."

"Well, I never!" Rose exclaimed. "That's not exactly truthful, is it?"

"It's a small deceit, pandering only to vanity."

"Like the business with the ruffles, I suppose. I was only trying to be helpful."

"If a customer wants ruffles, give her ruffles."

"Ruffles would make Mrs. Elverson look even larger."

"It doesn't matter what *we* think. It's what Mrs. Elverson thinks and is willing to pay for. Do you understand, Rose?"

Rose nodded. "I thought that selling would be little more than writing up orders, but I can see there's a lot more to it than that. It's learning how to deal with people, isn't it?"

Mrs. Sweeney beamed at Rose. "That's it, exactly. I knew you were a smart girl when I met you. Comb your hair and tidy up, then come back into the store and see what you can do to make our customers happy."

"Thank you," Rose said as Mrs. Sweeney ducked behind the curtain and disappeared. Mrs. Sweeney was a kind woman. Rose could hardly wait until Ma got here and the two women could meet. Tonight she'd write to Ma and tell her all about her new job and kind employers.

The store became so busy that Rose, without a spare moment for worry, relaxed with her customers and began to chat as she had seen Mrs. Sweeney do. She found herself discussing something she'd never even seen—a noisy new invention called the *automobile*. There were reported to be at least a dozen in Chicago.

"They don't need horses to pull them?" Rose asked in amazement.

"Horses! Oh, my dear, the terror those automobiles are causing in horses!" her customer said as she nodded wisely. "I've heard of two runaways and an upset carriage in which someone was badly bruised, all because of those noisy automobiles. Mark my words, those automobiles are nothing but a foolish passing fad."

Late in the afternoon, while Rose was thinking about automobiles and wishing she could see one, she looked up to see her brother Johnny with Mr. Sweeney at the counter. Rose started forward to greet her brother, but Mr. Sweeney handed Johnny an envelope, which he quickly slipped into his coat pocket before turning to leave the store without so much as a nod to Rose.

*That's strange,* Rose thought. *Why wouldn't Johnny stop?* But it occurred to her that visiting with friends or relatives would definitely be frowned on during working hours. She returned to sorting chemises as to size and arranging them on the shelves.

The blue of the sky had deepened and the electric lights on State Street were bright by the time the CLOSED sign was put on the door and Rose began her journey home. She was warm with the praise Mrs. Sweeney had given her as she left. Rose had put Mrs. Elverson out of mind, and the only problem she had to contend with was her feet. How different her new shoes were from her boots! She was glad she'd be taking the State Street trolley most of the way home.

She arrived last, and with two hungry brothers and a father waiting, Rose exchanged her hat and jacket for an apron and began to cook the evening meal.

As they ate supper Rose told about her day and asked about theirs. Rose was concerned about her father. He looked so exhausted, his shoulders drooping as he hunched over his plate. After Rose had finished the washing up, she found Da sound asleep in his chair, copies of *The Chicago Times* and *The Chicago Citizen,* which Rose had soon learned was the official "Irish" newspaper of Cook County, sprawled across his lap and on the floor by his chair.

Rose heard footsteps on the stairs. She opened the door to find Kate and quickly held a finger to her lips and led Kate through the living room into the kitchen. Automatically Rose put the kettle on to boil.

"I can't stay long," Kate said. "I just thought I'd stop by and ask about your first day at work."

Rose was pleased by Kate's friendship. "I'm afraid I made more than my share of mistakes, but Mr. and Mrs. Sweeney were patient and kind."

The water in the kettle steamed, so Rose poured it into a pot that held a heaping spoonful of tea leaves and carried it to the table.

"Johnny and Michael said they were going to a meeting," Rose said as she poured the tea. "I'm guessing it was with the Clan na Gael."

Kate frowned. "Tim's at the meeting, too, but I'm afraid it's not the Clan na Gael. It's a splinter group of hotheads trying to raise money to fund Irish rebels. Every Irishman in the United States wants freedom and independence for Ireland, but not all of us are for going about getting it through violence."

"Ma is strongly against violence," Rose said, "and I am, too. I'm sure that a great deal can be accomplished through peaceful meetings and talking out the problem, even though it takes time."

"We're in agreement," Kate said. "The result can't be measured in months or years. It should be measured in the number of lives lost or saved. That's all that counts."

"I take it Tim doesn't see things the way you do."

Kate sighed. "Tim's not the kind you can convince of anything. I worry a great deal about him."

Rose stared down into her teacup. "Your brother is very nice," she said.

"That he is," Kate answered, "in spite of his stubborn, mulish ways." As Rose looked up and laughed Kate added, "Tim thinks you're very nice, too."

As she took another sip of tea she said, "No more talk about brothers. There's a party at Hull House on Saturday night. My Sean isn't too interested in the Hull House parties, but I've convinced him to care for the children and let me go. Why don't you come, Rosie? You can meet me there."

"Will there be dancing?"

"Maybe. Often people entertain with dances from their native countries."

"Will Tim be there?"

"I doubt it," Kate said. "He's not much for Hull House either. Of course, if he knew you were going . . ."

Half an hour later, as Kate whispered good-bye, Da snorted and snuffled, turning in his chair without waking. Rose settled at the table to write letters. She wrote a note to Rebekah at the address she had given her in New York City. She hoped her friend had settled into her new life easily. Of course, Rebekah had her parents with her and that must have offered comfort. Then Rose began a long, detailed letter to her mother. At nine o'clock she walked into her father's bedroom, picked up the noisily ticking alarm clock, and reset it a half hour ahead. She placed it next to her own bed before she woke her father and informed him it was bedtime.

As Da stretched, rubbing his neck and arms, Michael and Johnny came in the front door. Michael walked toward the bedroom, but Rose put a hand on Johnny's arm. "Johnny," she said boldly, "there's a party at Hull House on Saturday night. Why don't you come and bring Tim?"

Johnny shook his head. "You'll not catch me inside that Hull House, and Tim shouldn't go there either."

"Why not?"

"It's not in the best interest of our jobs or our future."

Rose plopped onto the arm of the sofa. "Tell me, Johnny, exactly what is your job?"

Johnny stood a little straighter and said proudly, "I'm one of Alderman McMahan's staff assistants, as is Tim."

"Fine words, but what do they mean?"

"They mean that we can be trusted to take care of some of McMahan's business, such as calling on his supporters and those with whom he does business, even collecting campaign contributions."

"Is that what you were doing at Sweeney's?"

For a moment Johnny looked startled, then he said, "You could say that. McMahan has done them favors, and they're grateful."

"What kind of favors?"

"Rosie girl, running a business in Chicago involves more dealings than you can imagine. There are business and fire inspectors, tax collectors—the list goes on and on. If McMahan can save the Sweeneys the bother and hassle and—let's face it—an occasional under-the-table payment, then they have a good reason to be thankful."

"It doesn't sound completely honest to me."

Johnny broke into laughter. "Honest? It's a good, workable system, and it suits me just fine."

"I still don't understand why you can't go to Hull House."

"Jane Addams is treading on the aldermen's toes with some of the things she's done in her neighborhood, which is in the nineteenth ward—Alderman Johnny Powers's territory," Johnny said. "Would you believe that a few years ago she made such a fuss about the garbage piling up in bins that the mayor appointed her garbage inspector of that ward!"

"But if she wanted to clean up the neighborhood, that's a good thing, isn't it?"

"Not when she captured a job that's considered one of the political plums Powers should have the right to hand out. Fortunately, Powers had enough power to get the city council to eliminate the job, and out she went."

Rose opened her mouth to protest, but Johnny went

on. "Poor immigrants live in the area around Hull House, and the woman is constantly sending them things they need. She doesn't understand that delivering baskets of food and toys is every bit as important in politics as providing bail and fixing court cases and taking care of funeral expenses and handing out railroad passes and all the other benefits an alderman gives his constituents. A basket of food can buy a vote."

"Johnny! That's so selfish!"

"It's politics, Rosie. And politics is something a girl would know nothing about."

"I know enough, from what you've just told me, and I'm surprised that you're involved in it."

"Would you want me to be a laborer? Don't you think I can do more with my mind than think about setting one brick on another?"

Rose threw a glance at their father. Had he heard Johnny's thoughtless remark?

Johnny lowered his voice as he explained, "The Irish have got a strong foothold in Chicago politics, and it serves us well. It's kept you from being a housemaid, hasn't it? I like the work I'm doing, and I've got my eyes on the future." He grinned. "Who knows, someday you may be calling me *Mayor* John Carney!"

Their father yawned, stretched, and lumbered to his feet. "Early to bed, early to rise," he said. "Good night to one and all."

Rose watched with an ache of pity as Da slowly walked from the room as though every bone in his body hurt.

\*     \*     \*

The week went by quickly. One evening Rose found her father hunting for the jar of money, and she explained her bookkeeping system.

"I put in more than I should last week, so I'm a little short," Da said. "I want to stop by Casey's and see the boys, so just let me borrow a bit, Rosie."

"No," Rosie said firmly. "Da, the sooner we can bring Ma and the girls to Chicago, the better it's going to be for all of us."

"You're right, you're right," he said as he slowly shook his head. "Well, I'll be off to see the boys anyway. The building I've been working on has reached the point where bricklayers are no longer needed. Maybe one of the boys will have heard of a contractor looking for men."

"Oh, Da!" Rose cried. "I'm so sorry about your job. What will you do?"

He smiled and patted her shoulder. "Don't look so frightened, Rosie girl. This is the way of it in the building trades."

"It's happened to you before?"

"Of course it has, and I'll do what I always do. I'll go down to the hiring hall each morning until something turns up. I've been giving some thought to putting a few other irons in the fire, so there's nothing to worry about."

As he turned to leave the kitchen, Rose put a hand on his arm. "I'll pray for you, Da."

He patted her hand and smiled again. "That's just what your mother would have said. Ah, Rosie, you're so much like her."

Rose hugged her father. "I miss Ma so much," she said.

"And so do I, daughter," her father answered. "So do I."

# CHAPTER SEVEN

❖ ❖ ❖

IN spite of her concern about her father, Rose couldn't help feeling excited every time she thought about the Saturday-night gathering. Kate had sent detailed directions through Johnny, so Rose took enough fare for two cable-car rides each way, dropping the coins in the pocket of her jacket. She set aside what would be needed for her share of the living expenses, then placed the rest of her weekly salary in the jar. She marked down the amount added and the total before she set off for Hull House on Halsted and Polk.

Rose was surprised at the dreariness of the neighborhood she entered. The streets around the crowded apartment houses were littered with trash and garbage, and even though the sun had given way to twilight, a few pieces of washed, faded clothing still hung from the lines that were strung from houses to fences like tangled spiderwebs.

"You'll change here to a Chicago Union Transit car," the conductor called to Rose. "There'll be one along in fifteen or twenty minutes."

"How far are we from Hull House?" Rose asked.

"Only about five blocks."

"Thank you," she said. She'd rather walk than stand on the corner and wait for the next car, so she set off down the street.

From the open windows of the apartment houses Rose passed floated the odors of hot grease, onions, and garlic, with an occasional unfamiliar spice that tickled her nose. Children ran past and around her as they played in the street, dodging occasional carts, and quite a few men and women, dressed in dark homespun clothes, sat on the steps of the soot-caked tenements, chatting or arguing in unfamiliar tongues.

Rose had walked at least three blocks when she heard a high-pitched wailing that sent shivers up her backbone. She looked in the direction of the sound and saw that a group of people had clustered outside the door of one of the buildings and a large, black, enclosed buggy was parked next to the curb.

People at the foot of the steps parted to make a path as a small, compact woman in an untrimmed coat and bonnet hurried up the stairs and into one of the crowded apartments.

Curious as to what was happening and wondering if she could help, Rose followed.

A thin, elderly woman, her white hair tangled, knelt on the floor, crouched over a small, wooden chest. Her wails had faded to small whimpering sounds as she clung to the chest with all of her strength.

70

Two men in stiff black suits stood behind the woman. They looked at the newcomer with obvious relief, and one of them said officiously, "We're from the County Agent's office, Miss Addams. We have orders to take the old woman to the County Infirmary."

"The poorhouse," someone in the crowd murmured.

"This was our last call of the day," the second man said. "We can't budge the old woman, and we don't want to carry her out screaming. Maybe you can talk some sense into her head."

"She has a name," Jane Addams said firmly. "Will you please use it?"

He pulled a form from his pocket and glanced at it. "Gertrude Bauer," he said. "We told her we'd come to take her where she'd be cared for, but she'd have to leave everything here. Then she started behaving like this."

Rose was so upset by the poor woman's fear that she broke in without thinking. "It's such a small box. Why can't she take it with her?"

"Because it's against the rules," the man said.

"Anybody going to a poorhouse hasn't got anything of value anyway," the other added.

"A photograph, a tiny memento . . . you can't imagine how valuable they can be," Miss Addams said as she bent to touch Mrs. Bauer's shoulder. "Don't be afraid, dear. You're not going with them," she said.

"Our orders . . ." one man began, but Miss Addams interrupted.

"Go back and tell your superiors that I guarantee Mrs. Bauer will be cared for," she said. She looked toward the wide-eyed faces peering into the doorway. "Please," she asked, "some of you who are Mrs. Bauer's neighbors, will you help her, too?"

"Oh, yes," a woman answered and shuddered as she said, "I didn't know the dear old thing was on her way to the poorhouse. That's the last place I'd want anyone to go—myself included. I can come up with a bit extra in a meal or two."

"I'll help," another woman said, and a boy said, "My ma often sends things to eat to Mrs. Bauer. She'll keep sending them."

As the men from the county left the room Miss Addams knelt beside Mrs. Bauer and smoothed her hair. "We'll all help you," she said. "Do you have any family we can send for?"

Mrs. Bauer raised her tear-swollen face and sat back on the floor with a thump. Her skin was so transparent that Rose could see spiderlike trails of blue lines under the surface. It was hard for Mrs. Bauer to speak English, but she managed, with a muddled mingling of German and English words, to say that her husband had been killed in the mines. She'd had two sons and a daughter, but all of them had died before they were fully grown.

Now that the county agents had gone two neighbors became brave enough to enter the apartment. As one helped Mrs. Bauer to her feet Miss Addams drew the other aside and asked, "Can you help her to comb her hair? To bathe?"

The neighbor nodded, so Miss Addams motioned to Rose and left the apartment house. "Thank you," she said to the people who still remained. "Thank you for helping."

On the sidewalk Miss Addams studied Rose, dressed

72

in her snug-waisted jacket, skirt, and sailor hat, and said, "You don't live on this block."

"No," Rose answered and introduced herself. "I live near Wabash, and I was on my way to Hull House to go to a party. I've just arrived from Ireland. I was hoping there'll be dancing because I love to dance."

Miss Addams smiled. "We'll walk to Hull House together, Rose."

As they skirted a group of children playing on the sidewalk, Rose said, "I don't think I really understand Hull House."

Miss Addams explained, "Hull House is my attempt to bring together the people who have come to the United States and help them learn to adapt to this country and to adapt to each other, living in peace."

They reached a large complex of brick buildings, and Miss Addams led the way past some of them into a building with a broad, pillared porch and large front doors with beveled glass that was decorated like a beautiful home.

"These are our offices, and my staff and I live upstairs," Miss Addams explained. "You'll find that in the other buildings . . ."

She was interrupted by a woman so upset her face was mottled red. "I'm sorry to interrupt, Miss Addams," she stammered, "but you need to know. That block of apartments with rats and raw sewage that we want to clean up—well, Alderman Powers is opposing us. He says he's not going to let a bunch of old-lady busybodies interrupt legitimate business operations! Not only that, he's got Hinky Dink to support him."

"Hinky Dink?" Rose interrupted in amazement. "What kind of person would be named Hinky Dink?"

"Michael 'Hinky Dink' Kenna," Miss Addams answered. "He's probably the most crooked of all the aldermen, controlling most of the vice in Chicago." She turned back to her assistant. "Don't let this upset you, Margaret. We won't let Powers and Kenna stop us. We'll take this to the entire city council, of course, but we'll also notify *The Chicago Times,* and we'll make up some handbills and distribute them all over the city. Call Mayor Harrison and make an appointment for me."

As Miss Addams outlined her plans, Rose saw Margaret relax. Miss Addams reminded Rose of Ma. She'd stand up to anyone who wanted to keep her from doing the right thing.

"I'm sorry for the interruption," Miss Addams said. "As I was telling you, in the other buildings we have a kindergarten for young children and classrooms where we teach adults everything from cooking and hygiene to understanding credit and using North American banks. We also have lecture halls, a small art gallery, and a dining hall." Her eyes twinkled. "The party will be held in the dining hall."

She pointed Rose in the right direction, and as Rose thanked her Miss Addams added, "Please come back soon. I'm sure you have some talents you can share with us. We have many volunteer teachers."

Rose ducked her head. "I'm afraid there's nothing I could teach anyone, unless it's the jig."

"Teaching a jig might be of interest to many. How about next Sunday afternoon at two o'clock? We've invited an international group. You can show them some Irish dances.''

"There'll be Irish music?"

"Our fiddler can play music from any country.''

"I'll be here," Rose said.

She found the dining hall easily. Kate and Tim were waiting for her, and Tim smiled as she walked toward them.

The party was not what Rose had expected, but she was delighted. The guests had come to entertain one another with dances and songs from their native countries, and some of them wore amazing costumes. Two husky men from Greece wore short white pleated skirts and flopping tassels on their shoes. There was food from Italy, Sweden, Poland, and Greece; some of it tasted delicious, some of it a little strange.

Kate knew many people and kept introducing Rose to them. The festive feeling reminded Rose of the night on board ship when she and Rebekah and Kristin joined the celebration of immigrants who had come from many countries. If only Rebekah and Kristin could be here tonight! Wouldn't they love this party!

Having Tim at the party made Rose's heart beat so fast she knew it meant something special, and when it was over and he was helping Rose with her jacket, he whispered, "You are the prettiest girl here tonight."

Delighted, Rose smiled up at him. "I'm glad you came. Johnny didn't think you would."

"Johnny and Alderman McMahan don't go along with all Jane Addams *does,* and I don't agree with all she *says.* You can't have peace until after you've won what you've been fighting for." Quietly, he added, "But I didn't come because of Jane Addams."

Rose felt her face flush and quickly changed the subject. "I've been asked to come here a week from Sunday and teach the jig."

"Will you want a partner? I like to dance."

"Do you? Wonderful!"

Tim took her hand and for just an instant held her fingertips to his lips. "I'll come and dance with you, Rosie."

"Thank you," Rose managed to stammer and tried to hide her confusion. "Then I'll see you next week."

"Sooner than that," he replied cheerfully. "I'm going to escort you home after we drop off Kate."

The three took the cable car to Kate's house, then said good night. They waited for the trolley to take Rose home, so it was late—after eleven o'clock—when they reached Rose's house. A light glowed from behind the drawn curtains in the parlor.

Rose glanced up and said, "Da must be waiting up for me. Would you like to come in?"

"Not tonight," Tim said. "It's late. But I'll be here to take you to the dancing a week from tomorrow, and I'll visit with your family then."

"Thank you for taking me home." Rose looked up at him.

In answer Tim leaned down and lightly kissed her cheek.

Rose turned and ran up the steps, flinging open the door and leaning against it. She knew a man didn't kiss a woman—even on the cheek—unless the two of them were so serious they were talking about marriage. Rose was surprised that the idea of marriage to Tim Ryan didn't seem strange at all. She quickly pushed those thoughts from her mind. She was years away from marriage—or was she?

For an instant Rose felt nervous about what Ma would think of such shocking behavior, but then she remembered the touch of Tim's lips on her face and smiled. Rose had liked being kissed by Tim Ryan, and there was really no need for Ma, or for anyone else, to be told.

# CHAPTER EIGHT

❖ ❖ ❖

R OSE looked around the house to find that Da wasn't home and neither was Johnny, although Rose could hear Michael's growling snores coming from the room he shared with his brother.

In the kitchen, Rose found a stack of unwashed dishes in the sink. She worked quickly, cleaning up, and within a short time order had been restored. As Rose turned to hang up the damp dish towel her foot struck something. She bent down to pick it up. What was a potato doing in the middle of the kitchen floor?

With a sinking heart Rose tugged out the sack of potatoes and reached inside, pulling out the glass jar and dumping its contents into her lap. She well remembered the total she had written after she'd made her own addition earlier, and after her count she discovered the amount was short by three dollars.

Sick at heart, she clutched the jar to her chest. It was Da who had taken the money. She was sure of it. Her father was lonely for her mother. He had said he was. Rose knew he was. How could he possibly throw away the money meant for Ma's passage to the United States?

Rose heard the front door open and close. In a few minutes Johnny appeared in the kitchen doorway.

"You're home safe and sound, I see, but what are you doing down there on . . . ?" He broke off as he saw the empty jar and the money in her skirt. "It looks as though Da finally found your hiding place."

"He took *three dollars*."

Johnny sat cross-legged beside her. He pried the jar from her arms and stuffed the money back inside it. "Rosie," he said, "don't sound so tragic. It isn't the end of the world."

"How much longer is it going to take us to save the passage money if Da uses it to buy whiskey?"

"You, Michael, and I will make up the difference. We did it for *you*."

Anger welled up, a bitter taste in her mouth. "Making up the difference is not the same. Don't you see? It's as though he doesn't care enough about Ma."

Johnny put a hand on her shoulder, and for a change his eyes were solemn. "You can't see inside Da's heart and mind, Rosie. You've no right to judge him."

"I'm so terribly lonely for Ma!"

"So is Da. But he's lonely, too, for Ireland. He was a property owner there, a farmer who knew and loved the land."

"Michael told me practically the same thing, but that doesn't excuse Da from taking money to buy whiskey."

"No, it doesn't excuse him."

Rose slumped, and tears came to her eyes. "What should we do about this, Johnny? What would Ma do if she were here?"

"To begin with, Ma would find a better hiding place." The twinkle came back to Johnny's eyes, and he rested an arm around Rose's shoulders.

"And then?"

"That's the part I don't know, so why don't you just work on the first part? I'll walk down to Casey's right now and bring Da home. You get to bed, Rosie. The way you feel, it will be better if the two of you have nothing to say to each other tonight."

Rose gave her brother a quick hug and carried the jar to her bedroom. Earlier, Rose had discovered that the wardrobe had a false bottom. Now she pried up one end and found there was a space just wide enough to hold the money jar, if the jar were laid on its side. She tucked the board back in place and examined it. She could relax. No one could guess that the jar was hidden there.

But even after Rose had turned out her bedroom lamp and gone to bed, she couldn't sleep. As she lay awake she heard footsteps move up the stairs and enter the parlor. One set was sure and quick; one set was heavy and stumbling.

"Judge not lest ye be judged." Rose had heard her teacher, Sister Rita, say this often. She tried her best to soften her heart toward her father, finding comfort in reminding herself that time would pass quickly and soon Ma and the girls would come.

\*     \*     \*

The next morning Da could eat no breakfast and begged off going to Mass, returning to bed with a monstrous headache.

He looked so miserable that Rose brought him a cold cloth for his forehead. She walked to St. Columbanus with Johnny and Michael, who held a noisy discussion about the necessity of collecting money to fund an insurgent group in Ireland.

Rose didn't involve herself with their conversation. She had enough to think about. Somehow, she had to make Da understand how she felt about what he was doing.

Da had regained his appetite by the time Rose served the noon meal, and although he glanced contritely at Rose now and again, he said nothing. Rose, unsure of how she should react, didn't refer to the episode either.

Immediately after the meal both Michael and Johnny left the house. Where Johnny was off to was anyone's guess, but Rose supposed that Michael was on his way to see his Ellen.

The sky was gray, with on-again, off-again showers. Rose stayed indoors, using the time to take care of the family's mending and to bake bread ahead for the next few days.

To her surprise her father was in a good mood and asked her to play a game of draughts. "Checkers, it's called here in America," he told her as he put out the board.

As they played, Rose remembered games like this she'd played with Da in their home in Ireland. Had it been so long ago? The kitchen had been fragrant with smoldering peat and Ma's soups simmering at the back of the stove, and Rose had felt so loved.

After her father had won three games to two, Rose leaned back in her chair and said, "Da, I'm going to teach Irish dancing at Hull House next Sunday afternoon. Why don't you come and watch me?"

He looked pleased. "Are you that fine a dancer then, Rosie girl?"

Rose laughed as she stood up and lifted her skirts above her ankles. "I'll show you. Just pretend there's music," she said, and her heels and toes beat out a rapid tattoo.

A sudden thumping came from below them, and a muffled voice shouted, "What's all the noise about? What's going on up there?"

Rose flopped into a chair, giggling. "It's easy to see that the Horbowys don't appreciate the Irish jig—at least when it's taking place over their heads."

Da smiled. "You take after your mother, Rosie. When she was young, Maura was always the fine dancer. Other dancers would stop just to watch her."

"Da," Rose said softly, "let's do everything we can to bring Ma here as soon as possible."

"Of course, Rosie," her father answered, but he looked down at the draughts board, fumbling with the pieces as he packed them inside their box.

"With the three steerage fares and the twenty-five dollars apiece, it's going to take every cent we can spare." She hoped and prayed she hadn't sounded like a scold.

Da's eyes looked misty. "All morning I've been blaming myself and hating myself for what I did yesterday. But I thought if I met with the boys I'd find out who might be hiring—there's something I've set my mind to find out about—and you know that when they're buying rounds I have to pay my own share. I'd be ashamed not to."

Rose realized she should have expected excuses. "It's all right, Da," she managed to say.

"No, it's not all right, Rosie, and I'll be the first to admit it," he declared. "But I promise you just what I promised myself—I'll never again take so much as a penny of that passage money. Believe me, Rosie. Please, believe me."

"I believe you, Da," Rose said firmly.

Her father smiled the way a naughty child would smile once he'd been forgiven. As he pulled out a handkerchief to wipe his eyes, Rose thought, *I believe you, not because of your promises, but because I'm going to make sure you'll never find that jar of money again!*

# CHAPTER NINE

❖ ❖ ❖

D URING the following week Da was hired to lay brick by the contractor for a building being constructed on Michigan Avenue. He came home promptly each night, he turned his paycheck over to Rose on Saturday night, and she felt guilty that she had ever doubted him.

Early the following Sunday afternoon, Tim arrived. Rose enjoyed his surprise when she announced, "Not only are we lucky to have my father come along, but Michael and Ellen are going to join us there."

"That's good news," Tim said politely, but as Rose's father put on his coat and hat, Tim secretively reached for Rose's hand and squeezed it tightly.

Rose quickly pulled her hand away, but she smiled up at him, enjoying his boldness.

The afternoon was filled with laughter and music, and Rose was giddy with the joy of the applause. She had never danced so well with anyone as she had with Tim.

"You're the best dancer I've ever seen," Tim told her. "You even make me look good."

Da danced, and so did Michael, although he was known in the family to be rather clumsy and not a polished dancer. Ellen, as his partner, was a good sport.

"A fine girl," Da said to Michael, obviously impressed. "You couldn't do better. When your mother comes . . ."

Michael interrupted, his eyes on Ellen, who was Tim's partner for this dance. "I wish we could marry now."

"You and Ellen are young. There's plenty of time. You know that in Ireland the girls wait until they're twenty-eight or twenty-nine to marry. Why, your mother and I . . ."

"Da, they wait so long because there's such poverty. It's different here."

"When your mother comes." Da began again.

Michael nodded. "Yes. We'll bring Ma and the girls here first. Ellen and I have agreed to that."

Rose saw Ellen glance over at Michael and smile as though he were the only man in the room. She vowed that she'd be extra careful with her salary so that Ma could come all the sooner.

A Bavarian polka was called. It had a quick beat and, after a quick instruction in the step from the fiddle master, Rose found herself paired with Tim, caught in the fast-paced beat, laughing as they whirled and turned. When the music stopped she collapsed against him, and his arm on her waist slid to encircle her.

A heavy hand dropped to her shoulder, and her father's voice boomed in her ear, "The next dance is mine. I'm not too old to prance around the room the way the rest of you are doing."

It was the last dance, because five-thirty—the end of the dancing lesson—had arrived. As Rose slipped on her jacket she saw Jane Addams pause in the doorway, and she hurried to thank her for her invitation.

"I'm sorry I didn't get to see you dance," Miss Addams said. "Everyone seems to have had a wonderful time." She nodded toward a middle-aged couple and smiled. "Don't tell me that you were able to teach the Irish jig to Mr. and Mrs. DiFiorno!"

Rose chuckled and said, "There are people here from so many faraway places."

"This is a small sample of what world peace could be," Miss Addams said, "with everyone forgetting about differences in language and customs in order to share enjoyment together."

"Do you really believe world peace will come someday?" Rose asked.

"Of course I believe." She rested her fingertips on Rose's arm. "Isn't it better to work for peace than to accept the alternative?"

"You and my mother—who is still in Ireland—have a lot in common," Rose answered.

Miss Addams smiled and said, "Come to Hull House on Wednesday night, if you can. We're having a meeting of our Young People's League. We always have an interesting speaker on current affairs, and everyone is encouraged to ask questions."

"I'm afraid I'm not too knowledgeable about current affairs," Rose murmured.

"Then you should be," Miss Addams replied. "You'll find many other young working girls in the group."

"All right. I'll try to come," Rose said. She felt grateful to this woman who seemed to offer so much.

Rose hurried to join her father and Tim. She soon found herself riding home on the cable car with her father, who firmly pointed out to Tim that it would be folly to waste the money to ride all the way to Rose's house and home again when she already had her father on hand to escort her.

Once they were settled inside the car and it had started up with a clanging of bells and a grinding of the huge clamp pulled up by the gripman, Da pulled a face and grunted, "A city's made of nothing but bricks and mortar and miles of pavement, and all of it held together with great quantities of noise. Sometimes I long for the open fields and all the green of Ireland."

He looked so wistful Rose tried to change the subject. "Did you have fun at the dance?" she asked.

"That I did."

"And did you like Kate and her brother Tim?"

"Kate's a fine girl, and Tim Ryan seems like a nice enough young man who's mighty interested in my daughter."

"Da!" Rose exclaimed. Her face grew hot, and she hoped that none of the other passengers had overheard him. "Tim is Johnny's friend. He's just being a friend to me, as well."

"It's a good idea to keep that in mind," her father said. "You have many years ahead of you before you even begin to think of getting married."

"I'm not thinking of getting married, Da," Rose murmured. "Not now, at least, and not to Tim Ryan." But as she said the words she blushed again and knew they might not be as true as they sounded. She wanted what Ma had—a loving husband and children—and she'd be a good wife and mother with a family of her own to care for.

Her father nodded. "Over the years I've met a number of young men like Tim Ryan. They're out to change the world, single-handed, if you please. Just keep your good sense about you where he's concerned."

"Let's not talk any more about Tim," Rose said.

Da let out a long sigh. "Ah, Rosie girl, at a time like this I suppose there are many things you should be hearing from your mother. A father won't . . . that is he can't . . ."

"It's all right, Da," Rose mumbled. "Ma's already said them."

Her father sat up a little straighter and smiled with relief. "Well, then, that's that," he said. "Let's talk about your birthday. Only six more days, you know. We're going to make it a special day."

"Oh, Da, you don't need to," Rose protested, but she was thrilled that her father wanted to give her a wonderful day. She felt as excited as though she were a child.

On Wednesday evening Rose took the cable car to Hull House after work. As she entered the room where the Young People's League was to hold its meeting, she felt shy among so many strangers, but people near her began to chat with her.

The president of the group rapped for order, the audience quickly took seats, and the speaker was introduced.

Mr. Benjamin Rish was from one of the eastern universities, and the girl sitting next to Rose whispered, "Socialist."

Rose was surprised. "Are all . . . ?" she began, but the girl shook her head.

"Miss Addams believes in freedom of speech. We hear every kind of political thought. It's just that the socialists are leading the way in reform of working conditions."

Mr. Rish began speaking about terrible working conditions in the factories, and Rose was shocked at what she heard about working hours of twelve to fourteen a day, lack of safety measures, and poor equipment.

A woman held up her right hand, on which two fingers were missing. "This happened the first day I began work in a cotton mill. I was thirteen," she said. "They gave me little instruction in how to use the equipment and blamed me for carelessness."

While members of the audience asked question after question and spoke of unions, strikes, and reform, Rose listened. She wondered if these conditions existed in all cities and was grateful for her own good fortune in working for the Sweeneys.

The next evening Johnny burst into the house just before dinner, tossing his derby at the hat rack and grabbing Rose's arm. "Eat fast!" he said. "Tonight you're going with Alderman McMahan and Tim and me to deliver baskets."

"I have the kitchen to clean and mending to do," Rose insisted.

"Let it wait. You need to see how happy an alderman can make his constituents. You wanted to know what I do, so come and see. No arguments, Rosie girl. You're going with us."

Rose scarcely had time to gobble the meal and put on her jacket and hat before Johnny pulled her out the door. They took a cable car uptown and Johnny led Rose to a large, ornate brick building where Alderman McMahan had his office.

A broad-shouldered, portly man with more hair in his sideburns than on top of his head greeted Rose. McMahan said to Johnny in a booming voice while energetically pumping her hand with his large, plump one, "You're a fortunate lad to have such a beautiful, charming sister."

Rose remembered her manners. "Thank you, sir, for helping me find such a fine job," she said. "The Sweeneys are good people to work for."

Alderman McMahan beamed. "Anything I can do to help my friends," he said. "Anything at all. They need only ask."

When Tim arrived, his first smile was for Rose, and she was glad she had come.

"I've missed you," Tim whispered to Rose as they followed Alderman McMahan and Johnny out to a well-laden wagon.

"We were together Sunday," Rose said.

"It's still too long a time to suit me. I've never felt like this before."

"Hurry up," Johnny called to them. "Climb up on the wagon. Alderman McMahan will ride ahead in his carriage."

Tim firmly clasped Rose's hand, helped her onto the wagon seat, and smiled down at her in a way that caused her heart to beat faster.

It was all business, however, when they arrived in the neighborhood called "Back of the Yards." It was a cool evening, yet people still sat on the steps of the crowded soot-smeared houses, and children played tag and hide-and-seek among the trash bins.

McMahan jumped from his carriage as though he were a young man and began pumping the hands that reached out toward him. "I'm here to see dear old Mrs. McBride," he said to them. "I heard she was down with pleurisy and came as fast as I could to help." He snapped his fingers in the direction of the wagon, and Johnny leapt to the street, tugging a box filled with food from the wagon.

"Ah! You're a good man, Alderman McMahan," someone said, and others murmured agreement.

Rose was unconvinced. She realized the gesture was simply a trade-off for a vote.

She picked up her skirt and followed Johnny and McMahan up the stairs—Tim holding her elbow. The apartment to the left of the hallway was small and dark, but at least five adults were crowded inside it. On a bed at the far wall was a shriveled woman whose white hair flew in tangled wisps around her face. She peered out at them with pain-filled eyes, and Rose's heart ached for her.

McMahan praised her for how well she looked under such difficult circumstances, practically plumped her pillows, and presented her with a small cake that rested on top of the contents of the box Johnny had put on the table.

Rose guessed the men in the room were the woman's

husband and grown sons. They crowded around the box, exclaiming their thanks.

"You can always count on me," McMahan boomed. "As long as I'm in office I'm here to help."

Two of the men looked at each other, and one spoke up. "I got a ticket for leaving my rags cart in a place where they said it shouldn't be parked, although with the street so crowded, where else I could have left it I don't know."

McMahan clapped an arm around the man's shoulders. "Give me the ticket and think no more of it. It's taken care of."

The man's fingers scrambled through his pockets until they found and pulled out the traffic citation. "Thank you, Alderman," he said. "You're a good man."

McMahan laughed. "I'm counting on you to remember that when it comes time to vote."

"Oh, I will! We all will, won't we, lads?"

With another round of handshakes McMahan left the room, Johnny, Tim, and Rose following in his wake like a small parade.

Over and over they donated food gifts—to a family with a new baby, to a bride and groom, and to others who were ill or out of work.

Finally, the delivery work was over, and Rose, Johnny, and Tim left the alderman, a cloud of gratitude from his constituents still swirling around his head.

"Now, aren't you impressed?" Johnny asked Rose.

"I'm trying to sort it all out in my mind," Rose said. "The alderman wants votes, so he helps the poor. I don't like the way the things were given, but I realize those people badly needed help."

"That last part is all you have to think about," Johnny told her. "The reasons behind the donations aren't important."

"They are to the alderman."

Johnny laughed. "Rosie, there's no hope for you. You'll never understand the first thing about politics." Before she could retort, Johnny said to Tim, "I've got to stay at the office and bring the records up-to-date. Will you take Rosie home?"

"Gladly," Tim said. When they were out of Johnny's hearing, he confided, "I've been wanting a chance to be alone with you." He grinned. "Without your father between us."

Rose laughed and tucked her hand inside Tim's, not caring if she was bold. The cable car arrived, and they climbed aboard, squeezing together on one of the narrow seats.

"I haven't made up my mind about Alderman McMahan," she said. "Aside from handing out gifts and fixing traffic fines, what does an alderman do?"

"Each ward of the city has an alderman, and the aldermen make up the city council."

"So they help run the city."

There was no humor in Tim's smile. "The aldermen are powerful," he said, "and while they're in office they become very wealthy. They prosper from boodling and . . ."

"From what?"

"Boodling. Selling city franchises to businessmen is called *boodling*. You can't do anything in this city without paying off one or more aldermen. They control everything that goes on, including the vices."

Rose shivered. "How can you and my brother work for a man like that?"

"I won't for long," Tim answered. "The job I have with McMahan provides a decent living. He's allowed me to arrange my hours so that I take afternoon courses at the university." He smiled at Rose's look of surprise and explained, "It may take awhile, but I have plans to go into law."

"To be a barrister?"

"In the United States they're called attorneys."

"Oh, Tim, that's wonderful! When you learn all those fine legal words to talk judges into thinking the way you want them to, then maybe you'll agree that peaceful discussions are better than violence."

Tim scowled, and Rose held her breath, hoping that she hadn't ruined this beautiful evening by starting an argument. But Tim turned toward her and said, "Someday, Rosie, you won't be riding cable cars. You'll be driven down State Street in style in an automobile."

"Those horrible things that I've been told scare horses?" Rose laughed. "I've never even seen one."

The rest of their talk had no more substance than the wisps of clouds that skittered across the moon. They laughed, they teased, and Tim whispered compliments that reddened Rose's cheeks.

No one else was on the street when they reached Rose's house. At the front door Tim wrapped his arms around her tightly and kissed her long and full on her lips.

"We shouldn't," Rose whispered. "I hardly know you. It's not proper. My mother would be shocked."

"There's nothing wrong with a kiss."

"Well, if that's all it is . . ."

Tim interrupted. "That's not all it is, Rose. It's a way of saying 'I love you.' "

Rose's heart bounced, and she found it hard to breathe. "Tim! We have only known each other a short while. It's too soon to think of love."

"Is it?" he asked and kissed her again.

Rose had no answer. She melted like warm butter as she leaned against him.

# CHAPTER TEN

❖ ❖ ❖

ROSE was kept so busy by her thoughts of Tim, her
sales work at Sweeney's, and her housework at the
flat that the week rushed past. When a letter arrived from
Kristin, Rose tore the envelope open and read it eagerly.

Kristin's family had purchased a farm in a Swedish
community north of Minneapolis. She described the beautiful cities of Minneapolis and St. Paul, which didn't
sound the least bit like Chicago.

Kristin's letter was brimming with ideas new to Rose.
One passage was so interesting Rose reread it again and
again: "A group of women who live in those cities are
working hard to help women gain the vote. Father won't
even let me talk about voting. He strongly believes that
men should handle the running of governments because
women don't have the knowledge or the brains. Father
is going to have a surprise one of these days. As I told

you and Rebekah on board the ship, my father has no idea that I'm not the good and dutiful daughter he believes me to be!"

Rose was touched by Kristin's wish for Rose's happy birthday. "I haven't made close friends the way you and I quickly did on board ship. It's harder here. The girls my age are so predictable. I miss you, Rose," she said, "but we are not too far apart—little more than a day's journey. I do believe we'll see each other again."

Rose treasured the letter. She felt it was a wonderful way to begin her birthday.

Another happy surprise came when in honor of her birthday the Sweeneys put an extra dollar in the envelope with her pay.

"Buy yourself a special treat," Mrs. Sweeney said, but Rose knew the money would go into the glass jar and help bring Ma, Bridget, and Meggie to the United States even sooner. What did she want most for her birthday? She wanted her mother. She wanted the Carneys to be a united family again.

As usual, Rose was the first one home. As she bustled into the kitchen, tying an apron over her clothes, she discovered a note from her father lying on the kitchen table.

*Dear Daughter Rose, There's a special surprise in the ice box,* he'd written. *It's a taste of home.*

As a postscript he'd scrawled, *I'll be out for a short while but back in time for dinner. Peter John Carney.*

Rose opened the door of the ice chest and pulled out a large paper-wrapped package. Carefully she unwrapped it and found a beautiful golden-pink salmon—a whole smoked salmon!

Her mind flooded with memories of the delicate smell and taste of the salmon they often caught in the lakes at home, but a sudden thought sobered her. Here in Chicago this salmon must have cost a fortune. Where had her father come up with this much money?

Rose slowly laid the note on the table, pulled out a chair, and sat down to think. Something was all wrong. If her father had been here in time to bring the salmon, then go out for a short while—as he'd put it—clearly he'd not worked a full day. Had he been laid off again?

Where else would he go for a short while but Casey's pub? Rose put her head down on her arms and sighed. Her father had been different this past week. He'd really tried. She'd believed in him.

She got to her feet, rewrapped the salmon, and placed it back inside the ice chest. Slowly, reluctantly, she walked to her room, opened the wardrobe, and knelt in front of it. The loose end of the board rose on one side. Da hadn't even tried to cover up what he'd done by making the board lie flat.

She took out the jar, counted the money, and to her surprise discovered that an extra dollar had been added. Da hadn't taken anything out. He'd actually added a dollar to the amount in the jar!

Relief was short lived. Even if his job was over, Da should have come home with one full week's wages, and here was only one dollar toward Ma's passage money.

Rose rested her head against the hard edge of the wardrobe and murmured sadly, "Happy birthday, Rosie."

\* \* \*

Late that evening Tim and Kate arrived and Michael brought Ellen to celebrate Rose's birthday.

Laughing along with the others, Rose tried to hide her feelings. Finally, delaying as long as she could, she went to the kitchen to take care of the last-minute touches to the meal. She mashed some potatoes and boiled others, serving them in a cream sauce, along with a bowl of boiled and buttered carrot slices. She placed the cold salmon on a platter with chopped onions and wedges from the lemon she also found in the ice chest. Da hadn't forgotten a thing . . . except his promises.

Before the others joined them, Michael took Rose aside in the kitchen and whispered, "Why don't we wait for Da?"

"We've waited long enough," Rose said, fighting back the tears that burned her eyes. "We'll go ahead without him."

"But he brought the salmon," Michael protested. "It doesn't seem fair to go ahead with the celebration."

"What isn't fair," Rose said, "is where *his* celebration is taking place—at Casey's."

"Would you like me to bring him home?" Johnny asked from the doorway, but Rose could hear the reluctance in his voice. "I'll do it, if you want, but last time he wasn't too happy about it. He said it made him look bad in front of his friends."

"Leave him be," Rose whispered. "Johnny, get the others."

As soon as they were all seated around the kitchen table, Rose said, "Michael, if you'll say grace, we can begin."

Michael quickly bowed his head, murmured the

prayer, then immediately reached for the nearest bowl of potatoes.

Everyone ate hungrily. "The salmon is excellent," Ellen said, and Kate added, "I've never tasted finer."

But Rose found it hard to swallow. She kept listening for Da's footsteps on the stairs, hoping . . . hoping . . . but he didn't come.

When they had eaten their fill, Rose began to clear the plates from the table, but Johnny said, "Wait a minute, Rosie." He pulled a small box from his pocket and handed it to Rose. "It's a birthday gift."

"Johnny!" Rose pulled at the ribbon that was tied around the box. "You've never before given me a birthday gift."

"To be honest I wouldn't have given you one this year either, if it hadn't been for Tim," Johnny said with a grin. "It was his idea. He even picked it out."

"And probably paid for it," Michael said.

"Keep your suspicions to yourself," Johnny said as he winked at Rose. "What would Da think of a young man sending gifts to Rosie?"

A gift from Tim? Rose's heart pounded as she carefully lifted the lid of the box. With trembling fingers she unwrapped the folded paper that lay inside and gasped as she saw the heart-shaped gold locket on a long, thin gold chain.

Both Kate and Ellen admired it, but Rose stammered, "It's beautiful! But I can't . . . I can't accept a gift like this from Tim."

"I told you, it's a birthday gift from *me*," Johnny said.

"Johnny, if you . . ."

Johnny got up, took the locket from the box, and stood behind Rose, fastening it around her neck.

She reached up and touched the locket, turning it so that she could examine the engraved design that swirled around the heart.

"There's nothing inside it, if that's what you're wondering," Johnny teased. "If you want a lock of Tim's hair, you'll have to get it yourself."

Rose blushed so furiously the others laughed. She quickly glanced at Kate, but Kate's smile was warm and delighted.

As though to answer Rose's unspoken question, Kate said, "I think you're a good influence on my pigheaded brother, Rosie."

"Pigheaded, is it?" Tim exclaimed.

Rose lifted a hand as she heard quick footsteps clumping up the front stairs. "Here's Da," she said, but a loud pounding on the door startled them all.

Michael and Johnny sprinted toward the parlor, Rose and the others on their heels. Rose's heart pounded, and it was hard to breathe. Something terrible must have happened. Had Da been hurt? Was he ill?

Michael reached the door first and threw it open. A boy in uniform stood there. "Telegram," he said, "for Mr. Peter Carney."

"I'll take it," Michael told him. He signed a paper the boy handed him and accepted an envelope, then quietly shut the door.

Rose and Johnny silently waited as Michael opened the envelope and began to read. *It must be from Uncle Jimmy,* Rose told herself, remembering that Jimmy had telegraphed the time of her arrival in Chicago, but her hands were damp and she shivered with cold as she watched Michael's face turn gray.

"What is it, Michael?" Rose whispered. "What has happened?"

Michael looked up, his eyes dulled with agony, and said in a voice so hoarse it came out in a growl, "It's Ma . . . Pneumonia. Rosie . . . Johnny . . . Ma's dead."

# CHAPTER ELEVEN

❖ ❖ ❖

"**N**O!" Rose shouted. "It's not true! It's not true!" The room turned black, tipping and rolling, and Rose heard herself screaming over and over again, "No! No!"

A slap stung her cheek so hard that she gasped and opened her eyes. "Stop it, Rosie!" Johnny said and gave her shoulders an extra shake.

"Johnny," Rose whispered. "The telegram . . . it's a lie . . . Ma's all right. I've prayed . . . I've prayed so hard for her and for our sisters. Johnny, what they wrote isn't true."

"It's true, Rosie," he said firmly, and she suddenly realized there were tears on his cheeks. "You have to get hold of yourself now. Sit down. Kate's making you a cup of tea."

"I don't want a cup of tea," Rose said and burst into tears. "I want Ma."

"Rosie, you're not a child."

"Leave her alone, Johnny. Let her cry." As Tim gently took Rose into his arms, she pressed her hands hard against the pain in her chest, trying to force it away. Finally, her tears subsided, and she felt like the empty beach near Drogheda after the tide had gone out. Inside her was that same bleakness.

Tim helped Rose to the sofa and sat beside her, one arm still snug around her shoulders. She dried her tears on a handkerchief Ellen gave her and accepted a cup of tea from Kate. She took a long sip before she asked, "Did Michael go after Da?"

"That he did," Johnny said. He walked to the window and parted the curtains. "They're coming now."

"Bridget and Meggie," Rose asked, her head beginning to clear. "Who's caring for them?"

"The Doyles. The girls are in good hands."

"Da will have to go for them right away. How will we manage that?"

Johnny took a long, slow look at Rose, as though he were thinking out a new idea. "We'll manage," he said. "Don't worry about it."

The door opened, and Rose heard her father say, "Now, Michael, can you tell me what's so important that you have to make me come home in the middle of . . . ?" He broke off and squinted at the people in the room. "Tim . . . Kate," he said in surprise. "Ellen. How nice of you to visit. We're pleased to have you here." He gave a courtly bow that threw him off balance, and Michael struggled for a moment to help him remain upright.

"Ah, Rosie, I know! They're here for your birthday,"

her father said, his eyes crinkling as he smiled. "Well then, it's time to enjoy the birthday surprise."

Michael edged him into the nearest chair and put the telegram into his hands. "It's about Ma," Michael explained while Da confusedly peered and squinted at the telegram as though he couldn't make out the words. Michael took it from him and read it aloud.

At first the words didn't register, but as Rose watched in agony she saw her father's face sag, then crumple. "Maura, Maura, Maura," he whispered over and over, tears pouring from his eyes.

"Oh, Da!" Rose cried and ran across the room, dropping into his lap and holding his head against her shoulder. It didn't matter about the birthday. Nothing mattered except the horrible, painful news they'd received. Ma was gone, and what were they going to do without her?

Rose was up early the next morning. Like an automaton she dressed for Sunday Mass, then sat at the kitchen table staring at her hands and trying to collect her thoughts.

Johnny came into the kitchen and rested a hand on her shoulder. "Are you all right, Rosie?" he asked.

She barely nodded. "I'm making plans."

"What kind of plans?"

"The telegram from the Doyles said that Ma's burial would be taken care of, but it's only right that we pay them back, and we need to put up a stone. Her grave shouldn't go unmarked."

"That's right," Johnny said.

"So I've been doing some figuring. We'll need to borrow some money. We'll need to get round-trip steerage passage for Da and return passage for the girls and . . ."

Johnny sat down beside her and took her hand. "Rosie, listen to me," he said. "We can't send Da after the girls."

"We have to. He's their father."

"How will he cope with caring for two little girls on the ship?" Johnny's voice dropped, and he added, "At times he has difficulty caring for himself."

"Oh," Rose said, shocked that she had been so set in making arrangements that she hadn't seen the obvious.

Johnny's hold on her hand tightened, and he leaned closer. "Rosie," he said, "last night, after the others had left and you had gone to bed, I went to talk to . . . someone. I think we can work out the problem about the girls' passage. If all turns out as planned, there should be enough money to bring them home second class so they won't have to go through the examination at Ellis Island."

"How can you do this?"

"Didn't I tell you I have connections?"

"But who will bring the girls? They aren't old enough to travel alone."

Johnny shoved back his chair and stood, buttoning the coat of his suit. "Let me work it all out," he told Rose, "and then I'll tell you. For now, just relax. You don't have to do all the planning by yourself. You've got two big brothers to help." His smile was faint, like the fading ghost of his teasing self.

"All right," Rose said and tried to smile in return.

She went through the motions of attending Mass, walking home, and cooking their noon meal. She ate only because her father said, "Rosie, I know how much this

108

is hurting you, but the living have to go on living. Sit down and eat."

It was after Rose had washed the dishes and set bread to rise before baking when Johnny came into the kitchen and took her hand, tugging her toward the door. She could feel his undercurrent of excitement and see the spark in his eyes, and it puzzled her.

"Come into the parlor," Johnny said. "Tim's here. We've got something important to tell you."

Wondering at Johnny's odd behavior, Rose followed him into the parlor, where her father, Michael, and Tim waited for her.

Tim glanced at the locket Rose was wearing, and self-consciously she brushed it with her fingertips. Tim didn't know, but she intended to wear his locket forever. She would never take it off—never.

As Tim got to his feet and took her hands, Da cleared his throat loudly.

Rose would have liked to rest her head against Tim's shoulder, feel his arms around her, and cry away the pain that wouldn't let go, but she knew that her father's signal meant he expected proper decorum, so she pulled her hands from Tim's grasp and sat stiffly upright on one of the chairs.

Da's eyes were swollen and red. He blew his nose, tucked his handkerchief into a pocket, and said, "Rosie, Johnny and Tim have worked out a plan to bring the girls here right away."

"Now? Do you mean it?" Rose's heart gave a jump, and she looked intently from Tim to Johnny and back to Tim.

"I told you that it pays to know the right people,"

Johnny said proudly. "Alderman McMahan helped out—mainly by providing the right papers—and some of our friends have come up with the cash."

Rose gulped a long breath before she could speak. "You have the money? All of it?"

"More than enough," Tim told her. "In fact, we have tickets for Johnny in second class, not in steerage."

"Johnny? You're going for the girls?"

"It seemed logical," Johnny answered.

Rose was puzzled, because mischief shone in her brother's eyes. "McMahan was glad to give me the time off, whereas if you or Michael went after Meggie and Bridget you'd lose your jobs."

Da spoke, as if he hadn't been listening to what Tim was saying. "I'll have to get some things together. I can use the wicker suitcase Rose brought with her. If I . . ."

"Da," Johnny said, "it's better that you not go after the little ones. They won't remember you, and caring for them on the ship would be difficult for you. Think how much easier it would be if *I* made the trip."

Da hesitated, staring from face to face. "If you think this is right . . ."

"It's right, Da," Johnny said firmly.

"So it's all settled," Tim added.

Rose glanced at him quickly. That odd excitement in Johnny's manner—Tim had it, as well. What was it all about?

"This money loaned for the trip—it must be quite a large amount," Rose said. "How soon will we have to pay it back?"

"It's not a loan. It's a gift," Tim said.

"Better it were a loan," Rose said, an uneasy feeling

tickling the back of her mind. "A gift often comes with strings attached. Why would the alderman and your other friends do this for us?"

Johnny smiled easily, and he explained, "It's the political system. It works like this: You do a favor for me. Then someday you need a favor done, and you call on me, and I come through. It's as simple as that."

"So there *are* strings."

Johnny and Tim threw each other a brief glance before Tim said, "Rosie, here in Chicago the system works. Fines for overparking a cart or buggy are fixed, jobs are given out, even doctors' bills are paid . . . all in exchange for votes."

"These friends of yours would put out all that money in exchange for only three votes?"

With an indulgent chuckle Johnny said, "Trust Tim and me to know what we're doing. I'll leave tomorrow, and I'll return in less than two months with our little sisters."

Rose thought about it. Whatever political shenanigans her brother wanted to be involved in were his business. All she was concerned with was seeing Bridget and Meggie again. Think how lost they must feel, how much they must need her. Just think how much she needed them. She murmured, "Thank you, Johnny . . . and Tim."

# Chapter Twelve

✧ ✧ ✧

THE next morning Rose awoke as usual to the jangle of the alarm clock and had a hot breakfast on the table by the time her father and brothers arrived in the kitchen.

Johnny had already packed, so he wolfed down his breakfast, jumped to his feet, and pulled on his coat.

Rose hugged him, tears in her eyes. "God go with you," she said. "May He keep you safe."

"He will," Johnny answered softly, but Rose could feel a tension in his back and arms as though they were strung with vibrating wires, and she stepped back to study his face.

His smile was the same, but the excitement that had puzzled her earlier was once again in his eyes. "What is it, Johnny?" Rose asked.

"What is what?"

113

"Is there something you're not telling me?"

He laughed at this and turned away, stooping to pick up his suitcase. "There's nothing to tell," he said. "Is there a message you want to send to the little girls?"

"Yes," Rose said. "Tell them I love them. Oh, Johnny, they're going to need so much comforting." She gasped as a disturbing thought struck her. "Their clothes! Bridget and Meggie will need the right clothes to wear if they're going to travel in second class."

"I'll take care of it."

"I wonder if Sweeney's . . . No, their prices are too high . . . Maybe secondhand clothes . . . Perhaps I could ask . . ."

"Rosie! Stop blathering!" Johnny teased. "There's no time to get the girls' clothes, in the first place, and in the second place I wouldn't have room to carry extra clothing, not with two suitcases."

"Two suitcases? You have only one."

Michael pulled out his pocket watch and examined it. "Johnny's going to be late if you keep asking questions."

"But I don't understand," Rose said. "What is this other suitcase he's talking about?"

"A friend is sending a little something to his brother," Johnny said. His tone became teasing. "It's a good thing I'm not one for nosing into someone else's business the way our Rosie is."

Rose had no chance for other questions. Da and Michael surrounded Johnny, hugging him and wishing him well as they walked with him to the front door. Rose began to scrape the dishes, murmuring aloud a blessing she hadn't had time to give him: "May the road rise to meet you and the wind be ever at your back, Johnny, and may the Lord hold you always in the hollow of His hand."

A short while later, when she arrived at the dry-goods store, Rose told Mr. and Mrs. Sweeney about Ma. In spite of her determination to remain calm, Rose's eyes filled with tears, and she couldn't hold them back.

Mrs. Sweeney, cluck-clucking like a plump hen in a barnyard, patted and shepherded Rose into the stockroom, where she put her to work tagging a group of newly arrived skirts. "Work here until you feel up to waiting on customers," she said. "I know how you feel, Rose. When my own mother died I felt as though I'd been abandoned. There's no other pain quite like it."

As Mrs. Sweeney left her, Rose gave in to the tears, soaking her handkerchief before she leaned against the wall, exhausted. She splashed her face with cold water from the basin, tidied her hair, and began to work.

She heard the store open and the chatter of customers, but she methodically wrote prices on tags and attached them to the skirts until the lot had been labeled. Then, hanging them on a wheeled rack, she rolled them into the ready-to-wear section of the store.

"Could you help me, miss?"

Rose turned with a smile toward the woman who had spoken. "Of course," she said. "Would you like to see the very latest in skirts?"

Before she lifted a skirt from the rack and displayed it before her customer, Rose caught Mrs. Sweeney's eye and was gratified by her quick smile and nod of approval.

There was a steady parade of customers during the morning, so Rose was glad when two o'clock came and

Mrs. Sweeney suggested, "Why don't you take your lunch break now?"

Rose hurried to the storeroom, retrieved her package containing an apple, bread, and cheese, and sat next to Mr. Sweeney, who had just finished his lunch.

There was a firm knock at the back door, and Mr. Sweeney slowly stood up, grunting and stretching. As he opened the door a thin young man stepped inside and said, "I'm from Alderman McMahan's office. I'll be taking Johnny Carney's place until he gets back to Chicago."

He handed Mr. Sweeney a paper, which he read. "Wait here," Mr. Sweeney said and drew back the curtain, letting it fall back into position as he entered the store.

"Paddy Reilly here," the man said as he grinned at Rose. "You're a pretty one with that bright-red hair. Are you new to Chicago, girlie? Would you like to see some of the sights?"

Rose didn't smile. "I'm Johnny Carney's sister," she said. "My name isn't *girlie,* and I'm not the least interested in the likes of you."

Paddy's grin vanished. "Sorry," he said.

Rose twisted in her chair so that she could turn her back on him, but she had time to see Mr. Sweeney return and hand an envelope to Paddy.

As the door closed, Rose stood and brushed a few bread crumbs from her skirt. "Johnny says I don't understand politics," she told Mr. Sweeney.

"I've never met a woman who does," he answered and smiled. "That's why they'll never have the vote."

Rose thought of what Kristin had just written. She

116

wasn't so worried about voting for herself, but she was curious about Chicago politics. "Mr. Sweeney, if you don't mind my asking, do you contribute to Alderman McMahan because you want to or because you have to?"

Mr. Sweeney's eyes widened. "There's not much difference, is there?"

"I think so. If you pay because you have to then it's like paying a bully not to beat you up."

"Ah, now you're talking about the way it is in Little Italy. The Blackhands mail off letters to any of the Italians who are doing well, promising death for them and their families if they don't deliver thousands of dollars."

It was Rose's turn to be amazed. "Don't the police stop the Blackhands?"

"They haven't seemed to be able to."

"Do the rich people really pay the Blackhands?"

"Of course they pay."

"Have the Blackhands ever sent a note like that to you?"

Mr. Sweeney shook his head vigorously. "No. The Blackhands deal only with their own. That's the way it is in most of the Chicago neighborhoods. The criminals find that they can throw fear into their own countrymen more easily than they could into strangers who might fight back. Their own are afraid to call the police."

"From the names I've heard, it seems to me that many of the aldermen are Irish. Does that mean the Irish aldermen ask for contributions only from the Irish?"

"There you have a different matter. The power of Chicago's aldermen extends over the whole city. Someone had to take charge, so the Irish stepped in. Although

117

some of the aldermen have other nationalities in their backgrounds, you might say that the Irish have always taken a strong hand in Chicago politics."

"Then they should run the city honestly."

With a slow shake of his head Mr. Sweeney said, "Look at it this way. There's many who think it's better to have the Irish where they are than if some other group controlled the city, like those Blackhand Italians."

Rose thought of Kristin's hopes. "If women could vote," she said, "maybe they'd elect honest politicians."

Mr. Sweeney smiled and looked at his pocket watch. "There's no time to continue this lesson in politics, Rose, and it's easy to see you don't understand the political system. Your brother was right. Politics is not for women."

Tim was waiting on the front steps for Rose when she arrived home. He held out a small bouquet of flowers, their stems wrapped in paper. While Rose unlocked the front door and they stepped inside, he said, "I stopped by your parish church and arranged to have Masses said for your mother."

"Oh, Tim! How kind you are!" Gratefully Rose threw her arms around his neck, the gold locket swinging against his chest. As he lifted her chin for his kiss she responded. Life in the United States was different. This wasn't Ireland, where women, with nothing but poverty in their futures, chose to wait many years until they could marry a man with his own land. She was falling in love with Tim, and with all her heart she knew he loved her, too. In a year or two, give or take, Da would surely agree to the marriage.

"Thank you for thinking of my mother," she murmured.

"I was thinking of you," Tim said. He took Rose's free hand and pulled her toward the sofa, but she tugged away.

"No," she insisted. "I need to put the flowers in water before they begin to wilt and, besides that, it's time to start supper. Come into the kitchen with me."

Rose soon had coals burning in the stove and water boiling in the kettle. She dumped potatoes into the sink and began to scrub and peel them, working fast, trying to keep herself from being so aware of Tim and her longing to return to his arms.

As she settled the heavy pot of potatoes on the back of the stove, Tim stepped up and took her shoulders, spinning her around to face him. "Rosie," he said, "what are you doing?"

Rose sighed and looked directly into Tim's eyes. "I am trying to keep myself from thinking that more than anything else I would like to be kissed by you."

"Is being kissed so bad?" Tim's eyes twinkled.

"Tim," Rose said, mustering all her courage, "I'm falling in love with you." She thought she noticed him suck in his breath, but she hurried on before he could speak. "I'm too young for marriage. Maybe when I'm eighteen Da will agree, but surely no sooner."

"That's no problem," Tim said softly. "We can wait." His smile was slow and warm as he added, "Oh, Rosie, I love you, too."

Rose eagerly walked into his arms, but at that moment the front door opened and Michael called out, "Rosie? Are you home?"

She pulled away from Tim, nervously smoothing her

hair and her apron, afraid that Michael would be able to see the blush that warmed her face.

Michael, however, came into the kitchen intent only on the basin and pitcher in the corner. He noisily splashed water on his face and lower arms, puffing and snorting until he grabbed the towel hanging on a nail next to the basin and rubbed his face dry.

It was only then that he gave Rose a searching look. Patting her shoulder tenderly he said, "I see you made it through the day, Rosie girl."

"Yes," Rose answered. "The Sweeneys were very kind, and Tim . . . Tim arranged to have Masses said for Ma."

Michael shook Tim's hand, grasping it with both of his. "That's good of you," he said. He sprawled into the nearest chair with a sigh. "These are not only sorrowful times. We'll none of us be able to relax until we get word that Johnny got through safely and is ready to bring Bridget and Meggie home."

Rose caught the sharp look that Tim gave Michael. "Would you like to tell me what you mean about Johnny getting through safely?" she asked.

Michael's face grew red, and he picked at the edge of the cotton tablecloth. "Ah, Rosie, you know . . . what with storms at sea and all that . . ."

"That's not what you were talking about," Rose insisted as she turned toward Tim. "Part of love is truth," she said. "Tell me the truth."

"The truth," Tim said, "must not go out of this room. The more people who know about it, the more danger is involved."

Rose leaned against the sink for support, scarcely able to breathe as Tim continued. "Johnny is serving as a courier, delivering to the Irish Republican Brotherhood the money raised to help the cause."

Rose's voice came out raspy and dry. "Smuggling money! Johnny could be caught by the British and sent to prison." She closed her eyes. "He could even be killed."

"Don't take on so, Rosie," Michael said. "Nothing bad is going to happen to Johnny."

"Who else knows about this?" Rose demanded.

"Only the lads who helped arrange it," Tim answered.

"And maybe a few of those close to them." Michael's voice was low and apologetic. "Like Ellen."

Tim lowered himself into a chair. "You weren't to tell anyone."

Indignantly, Michael raised his head. "You told Rosie."

"That was different."

"No, it wasn't."

"Rosie's Johnny's sister. She was the only one in his family who didn't know. She had the right."

"You mean Da knew, too?" Rose asked. "And he let Johnny go?"

Tim got to his feet and gripped Rose's shoulders. "Listen to me," he insisted. "You don't understand the whole picture. We have to think of Ireland first and put our own concerns last."

Rose jerked from his grasp. "The money will be used to buy bombs and guns, isn't that right?"

"Of course," Michael began. "That's what . . ."

Rose ignored him, never taking her eyes from Tim's as her anger grew, swelling inside her chest and throat until she was choked with its heat. "You would willingly kill innocent people and say you're helping Ireland? What fools you are!"

There was anger in Tim's voice, too. "And what about the deaths the British have caused? You and those like you who keep saying that things will work out, that peaceful solutions will be reached—have you no love of your home country? Can you simply close your eyes to the crimes the British have committed against it? Do you want those crimes to go on forever?"

Rose slammed the palms of her hands against the table and shouted, "Killing people is not the answer!"

"It is if they're British!"

Furiously grabbing the front of Tim's coat Rose cried out, "You, Tim! You're Johnny's friend! How could you put your own friend in danger?"

"No one forced him. It was Johnny's own choice."

"What if he's caught and arrested?"

"He'd be a hero."

"A hero?" With all her strength Rose gave Tim a shove. "You send him into danger and call him a hero? No! He's a hothead without a brain—just like you and Da and Michael and all the rest who planned this terrible thing!"

"Calm down, Rosie," Michael said. "Don't blame Da. He had nothing to do with the planning. Everything was set by the time he found out about it."

Rose turned to her brother. "How about you, Michael? Did you help plan it?"

"Well . . . not exactly."

"I did," Tim said quietly. "When I first met you I told you I'd soon be returning to Ireland. Remember? I had planned to be the courier, but when we saw that someone from your family would have to go back to Ireland to get your little sisters, Johnny volunteered. It made sense. It gave him a good reason for returning."

Rose was furious ... she had trusted Tim. Bursting into tears she shouted at him, "Get out of here! I never want to see you again, Tim Ryan! I hate you! I hate you!"

# CHAPTER THIRTEEN

❖ ❖ ❖

WITHOUT a word, Tim left. Rose flung herself into a chair, burying her head in her arms as she cried for Ma, for Johnny, and for Tim.

Rose wanted to run after Tim, to tell him she didn't mean the angry words she'd shouted, to tell him that she loved him, but she couldn't. Tim had been responsible for sending Johnny on a dangerous mission, and Rose couldn't forgive him for that.

Michael tried to comfort her, clumsily smoothing her hair back from her forehead. "Rosie," he said, "I know how Ma always talked about peaceful solutions, but you're the only one who took what she said to heart. The rest of us know what needs to be done."

Rose didn't lift her head. She squirmed away from his touch and mumbled, "Go away, Michael!"

"I don't like to see you so miserable. I want to help you."

"I don't want your help! Go away!"

There was silence for a moment, then Michael said, "Listen. Da will be home in a few minutes. He's had it hard with losing Ma and being turned down for one job after another. You won't be rough on him, will you?"

Rose sat up and wiped at her eyes. She gave a long, shuddering sigh and answered, "No, I won't."

Encouraged, Michael said, "You know, there's no need to say anything to Da about any of this."

"I know. What good would it do?"

Michael backed a step away from the table. "So you're going to be all right now?"

"Yes."

He didn't move, and he cleared his throat twice as though he wanted to say something and couldn't. Rose sighed again and asked, "All right, Michael. What is it?"

"I was just wondering," he said. "You are going to cook supper for us, aren't you?"

Rose jumped to her feet and leaned across the table toward him. "Out!" she shouted.

Michael turned and stumbled from the room.

After Rose had finished the preparations for supper, she set places for two at the table, then took off her apron. As she put on her jacket and hat she called to Michael, "Supper is ready whenever Da gets home. I'm going out."

Michael appeared in the doorway. "Where are you going this time of evening?"

"Not far," Rose said. "I'm going to Kate's."

As she opened the door Kate held a finger to her lips and led Rose back to the kitchen where she'd been washing the supper dishes. "Pull up a chair," she said. "I'll have tea ready in a minute."

But Rose couldn't sit still. She picked up a towel and began to dry the clean dishes on the drain board.

"I'm glad you came by," Kate said. She slid a quick, concerned glance at Rose, and Rose realized how swollen and blotchy her face must look. "Sometimes, when problems get to be too much to handle, it helps to talk to a friend. I found that out when my father died."

"I didn't come to talk about Ma, may she rest in peace," Rose said. She twisted the towel between her hands. "Well, I suppose what I want to talk about does concern Ma in a way."

Kate took the top from the china teapot and peered inside. "The tea's a little strong, but it's still good and hot," she said.

"I like it strong," Rose told her. She waited until Kate had seated herself across the table before she said, "Ma used to say, over and over, that no good would ever come of sneak attacks against the British. She'd say that talking out the problem, that peaceful solutions were the only answer. I believed it then, and I believe it now . . . at least, I think I still believe it, even though I may be the only one in the world who does."

Rose slumped back against the chair. If only she could completely unburden herself to Kate . . . but she couldn't. Even though Rose trusted Kate, Tim had said that for Johnny's safety, as few people as possible should know what he was up to.

Kate smiled. "From what you just told me I'm guessing that you had an argument with Tim. I know how persuasive he can be."

Rose stared down into the silky darkness inside her cup. It took a moment before she found the right words. "It's not just Tim. Da, Michael, Ellen . . . Johnny . . . they all feel the same way."

Kate reached across the table and patted Rose's hand. "There are that many and more who'd agree with *you*."

"Are you one of them?" Rose met Kate's glance.

"Of course I am." Kate reached for the pitcher and added milk to her cup, stirring the tea vigorously. "Tim, now . . . he looks at life a little differently than you and I do. He was seventeen when our father died and quite a young rebel even at that age. More often than not he was in trouble with the British law—nothing serious, praise be. Ma moved to London to live with our elder sister, Jenny, but Tim—who wanted nothing at all to do with the British—came to Chicago to live near me. Unfortunately, he found plenty of transplanted Irish in Chicago who share his views about how to regain independence for Ireland."

"I wish I could change his mind," Rose blurted out. She gripped the locket, which felt warm in her hand.

"Wishing will never make it so," Kate answered, "and neither will arguing. I know. I've tried."

Rose put down her cup, the tea untasted. "He thinks I have no love of Ireland! He thinks I don't care what the British do! But I do care! I want Ireland to be free as much as Tim does!"

Kate sighed. "The Irish and the British hate each other. The Serbians hate the Prussians, and the Greeks hate the Turks."

"When does it end?" Rose murmured. "Will it *ever* end?"

128

"I'd like to make you promises," Kate said, "but I can't."

One of the boys awoke and wailed from the front bedroom, and Rose got to her feet. "You're busy with your family," she said. "I didn't mean to keep you."

Kate walked with Rose to the front door and hugged her before she opened it. "Don't think unkindly of Tim," she said and winked. "There's no law that says people in love have to agree about everything."

In anguish Rose stared down at her feet. How terribly much she wanted to be able to confide everything to Kate, who thought that Rose's unhappiness concerned a lovers' quarrel that would soon be over! She desperately needed someone to reassure her that Johnny would be safe.

"If you want to meet with people who value peace as much as you do, then come to some of the activities at Hull House," Kate added.

"All right," Rose said, trying to sound confident. "I will." But she returned home feeling every bit as miserable as she had when she left.

During the next three weeks Rose kept Johnny in her mind and in her prayers, asking all the saints in heaven to add their prayers to hers as she begged God to bring her brother home safely. Desperately, she prayed, "And please, grant to all of us Your special peace."

There was no peace for Rose as troubles were added to troubles. It was late in the day, the second week after Johnny had left, when a police officer arrived at Sweeney's asking for her.

Terrified, Rose could only stare at him, bracing herself for what he would tell her.

The officer pushed back his tall, rounded helmet and rubbed his forehead while he studied a slip of paper in his hand. "Michael, Carney . . . he's your brother?"

"Yes! Where is Michael? What's happened to Michael?" Rose leaned against the counter for support.

"There's no need to be frightened," he said kindly. "A load of pipe shifted and fell, hitting your brother's leg."

Rose clutched the officer's arm. "How badly was he hurt? His leg . . . is it broken?"

"That I don't know. All I can tell you is that your brother was taken to Augustana Hospital."

*Hospital! No one ever went to a hospital except to die!* In panic Rose whirled to one side, then the other, crying out, "Where is this place? I'll go to him. Right now. My hat . . . Where did I leave it? It's somewhere here."

Suddenly, Rose was enfolded in Mrs. Sweeney's arms. "Hush, Rose, hush," she said. "The shop will be closing soon, and we'll see that you get to Augustana. It's quite a distance north on Dickens between Cleveland and Lincoln."

"Shouldn't I go now?"

Mrs. Sweeney looked up at the policeman. "It's not an emergency. Is it, officer?"

"Nothing was said about an emergency."

"Who told you to notify me?" Rose asked.

"Your brother, Michael. That is, he told the nurse who called the station, and the dispatcher told me."

Rose took a long breath and began to relax. "Thank you," she remembered to say to the policeman. "I'll get to the hospital as soon as possible."

With a tip of his hat the policeman left. Rose, unable to concentrate on her customers' requests, was thankful when Mr. Sweeney finally walked the last shopper to the door, turned the CLOSED sign to face the street, and locked the doors.

Rose, guided by the Sweeneys, rode the electric cars to the six-story Augustana Hospital, where they were soon directed to the room in which Michael sat propped in a chair, his right leg tightly wrapped. A pair of crutches leaned against the wall.

Rose ran to him, hugging him gently, as though he were a cracked egg. "Oh, Michael," she said, "are you in much pain?"

"It's not so terrible," he told her, but beads of sweat popped up on his forehead. "I feel like I did when I was a lad and Porric Clancy's mule took a good kick at me."

"I'm so sorry."

He smiled. "It's not a major break, just a crack in the bone. The doctor said it would hurt like fury for a day or two, then begin to settle down. I'll be on crutches for the next six weeks or more." His smile shivered from his face as he added, "Rosie, I can't do that. We can't afford it."

"You'll do what the doctor tells you to do," Rose said firmly.

Mr. Sweeney bent over to peer at Michael's leg. "How did the accident happen?" he asked.

"A load of pipe hadn't been secured properly. It shifted and came pouring down. Luckily, no one was killed, and no one else was hurt."

Eager to get her brother out of this stark, bare place, Rose asked, "When will they let you go home?"

"Whenever you sign me out," Michael answered. He put a hand on Rose's arm and lowered his voice, obviously embarrassed to have the Sweeneys overhear. "There'll be the hospital costs to pay—I think they'll let us pay some each week until it's covered—and the ambulance. I'll need an ambulance to take me home, Rosie. I'd never make it on the cars."

"It's all right, Michael," Rose answered, although her heart sank at this extra expense. How would she ever pay these bills? To make things worse, Michael's income would stop until his leg healed and he was well enough to look for another job. She'd be the only one in the family bringing home a paycheck.

Leaving Michael with the Sweeneys, Rose went to the hospital's office and made the arrangements Michael had suggested. She rode home with him in the horse-drawn ambulance, wincing at every jolt and bounce that caused her brother to suffer as she fought back a resentment of his employers, who were the ones responsible for the accident, not Michael.

"Why can't the construction company you worked for pay your medical expenses?" she asked Michael.

"Because that's not the way things are done," he answered.

"At Hull House I've heard some talk about unions."

"So far it's just talk," he said and groaned loudly as a wheel of the ambulance dropped into a rut.

By the time the ambulance attendants helped Michael up the stairs and into his bedroom, Michael's face was the color of bleached cotton, and his shirt was soaked with sweat.

"Lie down and rest," Rose said. "Did the doctor give you anything to help with the pain?"

Michael pulled a paper twist from the pocket of his

132

overalls. "Here's a powder," he said. "Half in a glass of water now, the other half later, if I think I need it."

Rose mixed the potion, watched him drink it, then helped him pull off his overalls. It took only a few minutes for Michael to fall into an exhausted sleep.

Rose ran downstairs to the Horbowys' flat and enlisted Mrs. Horbowy's aid. Sympathetically, the woman gathered up the heaping armful of afghan she was crocheting and carried it up the stairs, where she lowered herself into a chair, the afghan settling around her, and resumed her work.

The next stop for Rose was Casey's pub. The room was dim and so thick with tobacco smoke she could barely see through the haze. But she recognized her father's tall back and broad shoulders and made her way to the table where he sat with friends.

"Da," she said, resting a hand on his shoulder, "you're needed at home."

He started, staring up at her in surprise. "Rosie! You shouldn't be here!" he said, and his face flushed with embarrassment.

"Please, Da," Rosie said. "Come home with me. Now."

After a quick glance at Rose, the gaze of the other men at the table shifted away in deference to their friend. Da's voice grew rough as he said, "I'll not have a daughter be telling me what I can and cannot do. Go home, Rosie. I'll deal with this later."

"Da!" Rose insisted. "Listen to me! Michael was hurt on the job. It's his leg—a crack in one of the bones. They took him to the hospital, but now he's home, and I need you."

"Michael's hurt? Why didn't you say so in the first place?" Da attempted to rise, the first time falling back in his chair and upsetting what was left of his drink. Rose stood quietly, fighting back the impulse to hold his arm and help him to his feet.

As he finally succeeded, he stumbled into Rose and grasped her arm for support. None of Da's friends offered to help, so Rose led her father out of the pub and down the street to their house.

After Rose had thanked Mrs. Horbowy, who enfolded herself in the large afghan and left for her own flat, Rose took Da's hat and coat and hung them on the rack.

"While you were talking to Mrs. Horbowy, I took a look at Michael," Da said. "It couldn't be too bad, because he's sleeping like a baby."

"The doctor gave him something to help him sleep," Rose said. "Sit down, Da. We have to talk."

Da dropped into the nearest chair, which shuddered under him. Rose sat across from him, leaning toward him, and tried to soften the urgency she felt. "I know how much you miss Ma. We all miss her. Each day I see things that remind me of Ma—the way a woman walks, a flower Ma used to love—and knowing I won't be seeing her again hurts something terrible. I know it must be even harder on you, Da."

Rose reached out and took his hands in hers. "It's hard to keep going, day by day, but we have to. There's you and Johnny and Michael and me . . . and the girls. We have to help one another. Especially now."

Da raised his head and looked at Rose through red-rimmed eyes. "You're telling me to stop drinking. Don't scold me, Rosie. A pint or two . . . it's not much."

"You can't be at Casey's and here taking care of Michael."

"Mrs. Horbowy . . ."

Impatiently, Rose shook her head. "Mrs. Horbowy has her own work to do, her own family to care for. And I have a job to go to."

Da's smile was coaxing. "Michael needs a woman's care, Rosie girl. Something will turn up for me soon. I'm there where they're hiring each morning. I have an application in . . ."

"No, Da. We can't count on it. At least for now we can count on my job at Sweeney's. I need you to stay home and take care of Michael."

Still coaxing, his smile dimming only a little, Da said, "Now, Rosie, an occasional visit with the boys at Casey's can't hurt."

"No, Da. No more Casey's."

He leaned back in his chair with a great shuddering sigh and closed his eyes. Just as Rose was beginning to wonder if he had fallen asleep he suddenly opened his eyes and said, "Ah, Rosie, this tragedy of Michael's has clouded our brains. There's no point in trying to decide anything tonight. We'll think much more clearly in the morning."

Rose watched him struggle to his feet and leave the room. For a long while she sat, staring at her hands, wondering why her world of love and happiness had suddenly cracked and fallen apart, leaving her alone to pick up the pieces.

135

# Chapter Fourteen

❖ ❖ ❖

In the morning Da, filled with remorse, vowed to stay at home, caring for Michael, and not set foot outside the house.

Michael, who reported later that Da was true to his word, improved rapidly and claimed he'd be off his crutches and on the job again even before the six weeks were up. Ellen was eager to spend Sunday afternoons with Michael, happily catering to his every whim and trying to convince him that being a policeman would be far safer than going back to a low-paying, unsafe construction job.

Da quickly disappeared during these times—visiting with the boys at Casey's—and Rose spent her free hours at Hull House with Kate, strangely comforted in the presence of other people who not only believed in world peace but who actively did something to achieve it.

On the third Sunday a professor came from a large university on the East Coast to speak about Abraham Lincoln. If only the Irish had someone like Abraham Lincoln to lead them, Rose thought, how different their lot might be.

After the lecture Rose strolled to the car stop with Kate.

"How did things work out between you and Tim?" Kate asked. "Did you settle your argument?"

"I haven't seen Tim," Rose answered, the sudden pain of remembering causing her to stumble.

Kate took her arm, steadying her, and peered into Rose's face in amazement. "You haven't seen him at all? But that was three weeks ago!"

"I know."

Kate sighed in exasperation. "What's the matter with the lad? I've never known him to be stubborn or hold a grudge."

"Don't blame Tim," Rose said quickly. "I—I said some unkind things to him."

"That's a surprise. I thought the two of you were getting along so well."

"I thought so, too."

"Do you want to talk about it?"

"I can't," she said.

Her answer had been so abrupt Rose worried that Kate might be hurt, but Kate just smiled and squeezed Rose's arm. "You're right," she said. "Whatever has come between you and Tim is a matter of privacy. Just remember that I'm here if you need me, and I think I'll tell that brother of mine that he's making a big mistake."

The cable car rattled to a stop, and the two of them

climbed aboard. "No, don't tell him!" Rose said. She smoothed her skirt around her legs, embarrassed at her outburst of panic. "I told you, I'm the one who said the unkind things. What happened was no one's fault but mine, and maybe it's better that it happened, because Tim and I will never agree on the best way for Ireland to gain independence."

A chuckle escaped as Kate said, "There's much more to love and happiness than agreeing on the means to Ireland's independence! Did your parents agree on *everything*?"

"No," Rose said. "Ma was the peacemaker, while Da took the opposite side, with the boys."

"There. You see?" Kate said decisively, but Rose remained silent. The situation in which Tim had involved Johnny had gone far beyond a mere discussion of political action, and she could see no way to make things right between them ever again.

Rose arrived home late, hoping that Ellen would have begun making the supper. Cooking was ever and always a woman's lot in life, but sometimes Rose got awfully tired of the whole routine of planning meals, shopping, haggling over prices, washing and storing the food, cooking it, saving the leftovers, then cleaning the dishes and the kitchen . . . over and over and over again.

She was so intent on her thoughts that it took a moment for her to absorb the scene in the parlor as she opened the front door. The people within stood without moving, like a group of statues, each of them staring at her: Michael in his chair, his leg propped up on a hassock . . . Ellen beside him . . . Da peering up at Rose, his shoulders bent as though he'd been struck . . . and Tim. What was Tim doing here?

Tim was the first to recover. He strode to Rose's side and grasped her hand, as he closed the door behind her. "We've had bad news," he told her.

"It's about Johnny, isn't it?" Rose whispered, fear making her light-headed. She whirled to face Tim and clutched his arms. "What have you done to Johnny now?"

Tim winced, but his voice was steady. "Johnny was caught with the money at the dock and arrested by the British police."

Rose felt her knees give way, but she staggered back, dropping into the nearest chair. Never taking her eyes from Tim's face she whispered, "What will they do to him?"

"He'll have a trial," he said.

Rose felt the heat of despair and anger rising through her chest and neck to the top of her head. "You and your plan!" she snapped at Tim. "Now you'll have your hero!"

Da had missed the tone in Rose's voice. "Yes, a hero," he said, the pride in his voice barely overriding the pain. "Our Johnny's a hero, doing what any fine young Irish lad would do for his country."

"*This* is his country, Da," Rosie said. "Johnny chose to come to the United States to live."

Her father raised his head and blinked with surprise. "But Rosie girl," he said, "wherever he may be, an Irishman is always an Irishman and loyal to his country from the day he was born."

As Michael interrupted, Rose was shocked to see the pallor of his skin and the deep worry lines carved into his face.

"It's not fair of you, Rosie, to put the blame on Tim," he said. "Johnny has a mind of his own, and he was eager to go."

"Smuggling the money to the insurgents was Tim's idea."

"Listen to me, Rosie. Johnny will undoubtedly spend a few years in prison. How many years will depend on how much support the Irish press can muster for him among the people. It's in Johnny's favor that he wasn't armed."

"Armed!" Rose looked from Michael to Tim and back to Michael. "Thank the good Lord he wasn't armed! No one would . . ."

"Listen, Rosie! Two of the Irish lads *were* armed, and both were killed. One was a close friend of Tim's since boyhood."

"Oh, no," Rose whispered. She glanced up at Tim. "I'm so terribly sorry."

Tears glimmered in Tim's eyes, and Rose wanted to jump up and hold him and comfort him, but her legs would not respond, and she couldn't say the words of comfort.

Instead, she clapped her hands over her face and bent double, her head resting on her knees, and began to cry, all the tension and worry of the past three weeks dissolving into loud, aching sobs.

Rose would have loved to have an arm around her shoulders, a comforting hand in hers, but no one came near her. No one even spoke.

The force of the torrent had passed when suddenly Rose had such a frightening thought she threw herself upright and cried out, "Good heavens! What are we going to do about getting the girls?"

# CHAPTER FIFTEEN

❖ ❖ ❖

DA and Michael stared at each other before they looked back to Rose.

"Bridget and Meggie . . . Yes, we must think of Bridget and Meggie," Da said. "With our worry about Johnny . . ." The sentence faded away.

Rose struggled to her feet and turned to where Tim had been standing, but he was nowhere in sight.

"Tim left while you were in tears," Ellen said. "He feels terrible about what happened, Rosie. Before you got here he kept telling us over and over that it should have been him, not Johnny."

"That doesn't bring Johnny back," Rose said bitterly.

"As I said before, you're being too hard on Tim," Michael told her. "When he and Johnny . . ."

Rose held up the palm of one hand as she interrupted. Couldn't they tell how much this was hurting her and

143

how heartbroken she was about Tim? "Please stop!" she insisted. "I don't want to talk about Tim. We have to think about what we're going to do."

Pacing back and forth across the small parlor Rose tried to plan and speak at the same time. "Johnny had a round-trip ticket and the girls' one-way tickets in second class with him. Will the authorities let us have the tickets, do you think?"

"I don't know," Da said helplessly.

Ellen spoke up. "It would probably depend on how fair the person in charge wanted to be and how well he could be persuaded."

Da perked up and for the first time looked hopeful. "Ah, Rosie," he said, "you have a good way of putting words together to get what you want. The British police would listen to you, they would."

Rosie groaned. With all her heart she wanted to go after her sisters, but how could she?

"Da," she said, "I am the only one in the family with a job. We have to pay rent and buy food."

"I *want* to work," he began, but Rose interrupted.

"I know you do," she said gently, "and you're a good, hard worker, too. Ma was always proud of all you could do, but we have to be honest with each other about our situation. Michael's leg will take time to heal. He can't work, and he isn't able to get Bridget and Meggie. Da, you're the one who will have to go."

Her father's hands shook and Rose pretended to herself that she hadn't noticed.

"Me, Rosie?" he asked, then he dropped his voice as though he were speaking to himself. "It wasn't supposed to be this way, you know. Maura would bring the little ones with her when it was her turn to come over. That's the way we'd planned it. But Maura . . ." His eyes filled with tears as he said, "The girls need me."

She took a deep breath and said, "Da, it isn't just Bridget and Meggie who need you. Johnny also needs his father. He needs to know that you're there to stand by him and to see that he gets whatever and whomever he needs—a barrister, an advocate—someone who will help him get as light a sentence as possible."

"Do you really think I can do all this?" Da asked.

"Of course you can," Rose answered bluntly, "if you just stop drinking."

Ellen's gasp caused Rose's cheeks to burn, but she kept her eyes on her father. "You can do it, Da," she repeated firmly, in spite of the terrible doubt she felt. What other choice did they have? Da was the only one who could go.

"All right, all right," Da murmured. "I'll do as you wish, Rosie."

"Thank you," she said. What she really wished was that Da could be once again her strong, wonderful father—the father who could solve all her problems.

"What about Da's ticket across and the train ticket to the ship in New York?" Michael asked.

Rose wanted to groan aloud, to fling herself across her bed and let somebody else come up with the solution to the problem, but she said, "I've given the hospital the little we'd saved. We'll need at least fifty dollars, maybe more, so I suppose we'll have to borrow the money."

Ellen spoke quickly, staring down at her hands. "I've been saving a bit of money on my own for the wedding, but this comes first. You can count on fifteen dollars."

As Rose expressed her thanks, she caught the special, loving look that passed between Michael and Ellen. Although she was happy for them and grateful that Ellen would someday be her sister, she jealously ached with the loss of Tim's love.

"Who else do we know who might help?" Da asked.

They looked at one another helplessly until Rose said, "Johnny bragged about all the fine things Alderman McMahan could do and told us he'd even helped with this . . . this smuggling scheme. Maybe he'll continue to help by lending the rest of the money Da will need."

"He didn't give money," Michael said. "He only arranged for the legal papers Bridget and Meggie would need."

"Then he might even help with Johnny's legal problems, too," Rose said. "The least I can do is give it a try. If the Sweeneys will let me take an hour off tomorrow morning I'll visit the alderman's office and ask. Surely, it won't hurt to ask."

"I can give you an hour off without docking your pay," Mr. Sweeney said, frowning with concern, "but I hope you understand, Rose, that if you're gone any longer I'll have to deduct the time from your salary. It's only fair. Toward midday the store gets busy, and we'll need your help."

"I understand," Rose answered. "I'll go to Alderman McMahan's office right now, and what I have to say won't take long."

A short while later she entered McMahan's office and explained her lack of time to the same young man who had visited Sweeney's.

He looked at her as though he'd never seen her before. "I'll tell the alderman," he said pompously and vanished behind the heavy door that led to the inner offices.

Rose waited at least twenty minutes, now and then nervously glancing at the loudly ticking clock that hung on the far wall. She was surprised when the outer door opened, and Tim entered the room.

He stopped and stared. "Rosie?" he asked. "What are you doing here?"

"I came to ask the alderman to help Johnny," she answered. "I also need to ask him for a loan. We don't have enough money to send Da to take care of Johnny and to bring back Bridget and Meggie."

"Your father?" Tim blurted out. "You're sending him?"

Rose lifted her chin, hoping Tim couldn't see the blush staining her cheeks. "He's always been a good, loving father," she said. "There's no reason why he shouldn't go."

"I'm sorry, Rosie. I guess I meant . . ."

Rose slumped against the back of the chair. "There's a very good reason why Da *should* be the one to go," she said honestly. "Michael is laid up with his injured leg, and I'm the only one able to support us right now."

"I wanted to come and see Michael," Tim said, "but I didn't know if you . . ."

He didn't finish the sentence, letting the words rise as if he'd been asking a question, but Rose didn't answer. She looked again at the clock, and Tim asked, "Have you been waiting long?"

"More than twenty minutes."

"I'll see what I can do," he said, but he paused at the

door of the inner office and glanced at the locket that gleamed against her white shirtwaist. "Rosie ... about us," he began.

Rose's heart began to thump, and she tried to force it to slow down. "If I'm not back within the hour Mr. Sweeney will deduct the time from my wages," she told him.

"Then I'll talk to McMahan," Tim said quietly, and entered the inner office.

The door opened again in a few seconds and Paddy hurried out, throwing an anxious look behind him. Tim appeared in the doorway and beckoned. "Come in, Rosie. The alderman hadn't been told you were waiting to see him."

Rose went through a smaller office into a large room decorated with paintings of landscapes that looked as though they belonged in a museum. Alderman McMahan rose from behind a gigantic, gleaming cherrywood desk and gestured to a chair.

"Please sit down, Miss Carney," he said. "The sad plight of your brother Johnny has just come to my attention."

As Rose perched on the edge of a large, leather covered chair, McMahan lowered himself into his own chair and shook his head sadly. "You realize, of course, that I had no knowledge of his plan to smuggle money for that group he belongs to. You know about the group?"

"All I've been told is that it's made up of some of the members of the Clan na Gael."

He nodded sagely. "It's probably just as well that neither of us know much about its actions. I'm all for home rule in Ireland, but not the way these young hotheads are going about it."

Rose didn't believe him. His words were too smug and self-assured. She supposed he had to protect himself, but she didn't like the way he was lying in order to do it. She had no choice but to accept what he'd said. Through the open door she heard Tim clear his throat. Time was running out. She'd better get to the point. "Johnny needs help," she told McMahan.

"Ah, that he does. What a shame. He's a fine lad, a fine lad," he repeated. "How could he have gotten himself into such a fix? If there was only something I could do for him you can be assured I'd do it."

"There *is* something you could do," Rose said, suddenly encouraged. "Johnny will need legal help. He'll need a barrister, but we have no money to . . ."

McMahan interrupted, holding up a hand. "Oh, he'll get help from the insurgents and their supporters in Ireland. I'm sure of that. But as for me . . . well, I think you can understand that in my position I can't afford to become involved."

"You were involved in providing the papers my little sisters would need to enter the United States."

His eyes lit up, and he smiled. "That's an entirely different matter. Providing the proper paperwork to my constituents is part of my job. I can only repeat that I had no idea money would be smuggled to the Irish insurgents, and I had no part in this at all."

Rose took a deep, shuddering breath and clenched her fists, which lay in her lap. She knew about the paperwork he was so sanctimonious about, like fixing traffic citations, but she was well aware that she had to keep herself

149

in control. It was terribly important not to alienate the alderman. "Then please, Mr. McMahan, will you lend us the money for my father's train fare and passage to Ireland to get my sisters? We will pay every penny of the loan back with whatever interest seems fair to you. I promise."

There was a long pause while the alderman leaned back in his chair, rubbing his hand over the grooves in his face from his forehead down to his chin. Finally he straightened up, leaned on the desk, and said, "Miss Carney, I ask you, how would this look? You'd know and I'd know that the money was for your father's passage, but there might be some who would think I was supporting your brother's cause."

Rose gasped. "I wouldn't tell! No one ever need know the money came from you."

McMahan preened just a bit as he said, "A man in my position has his enemies. They know everything about me, from what I pay for my clothes to what I eat for dinner. It wouldn't take long for them to find out if I lent money to your family, and the rumors would begin."

Rose had a hard time keeping her composure. She fought against a dark cloud of panic and tried to keep her voice from rising as she said, "I don't know where else to go for help!"

McMahan hesitated just a moment, then said, "A word of advice from a friend. You'll find plenty of moneylenders in Chicago, but don't borrow from them. Their rates are so exorbitant you'll never be free."

He got to his feet and walked toward the open doorway. Rose stood, too, realizing she was being dismissed, and followed him to the outer office. He chatted pleasantly as he bid her good-bye, but Rose was so desperate she didn't hear a word he was saying.

A few minutes later she crossed to the block on State Street that held Sweeney's Dry Goods Store, but she paused outside a small jewelry shop, drawn to a card in the window on which was printed GOLD AND SILVER BOUGHT AND SOLD.

Rose touched the locket with trembling fingers. It was her last tie to Tim and to Johnny, and she had promised herself to wear it always.

Frantically, before she could stop herself, she flung open the door of the shop and stepped inside.

An elderly man scrambled toward her, squinting to see her better. "What can I do for you?" he asked.

Rose reluctantly removed the locket, dropping the chain into his outstretched hand. "Your sign says that you buy gold," she said. "How much will you pay for this locket?"

The man put on a pair of thick glasses and held the locket almost to his nose as he studied it. Then—to Rose's horror—he gently bit it. "No harm done," he said to her. "That's one way to test for real gold."

Again he studied the locket, looked up at Rose, and said, "Two dollars."

"Only two dollars!" Rose exclaimed. "It must have cost much more!"

"What it cost doesn't concern either of us. What you asked is how much I'd give you for it."

"It's not enough." Rose was sick at heart at what she had almost done. She held out a hand, palm up, for the locket.

"Two-fifty and no more."

"No," Rose said. "Let me have my locket, please."

"You won't find a better price anywhere else."

Rose stared at him. "I need at least fifty dollars."

The man laughed and dropped the locket into her palm. "Good luck," he said.

Rose fastened the chain of the locket once again around her neck and left the store, hurrying toward Sweeney's. What had she been thinking of? How could she have sold this locket at any price?

"I want my sisters." The words came out in a sob. Two people passing on the sidewalk turned and stared at her curiously, but Rose didn't care.

The rest of the day she worked like an automaton. All she could think was, *What should I do? Where will I get the money? My sisters . . . we must come up with enough money to bring my sisters to Chicago!*

# CHAPTER SIXTEEN

❖ ❖ ❖

THAT evening, after the Carneys had eaten dinner, Rose told Michael and Da about her unsuccessful meeting with the alderman. "I don't know who else to ask for a loan, do you?" she asked.

Da stared down at the table. "It would be no use to bring it up with my friends. Most of the boys have little or nothing to spare. It's hard to get jobs when each morning at the hiring site there's a large crowd of laborers and many of them are young, strapping lads." He sighed and added, "I've been looking into something I hope will work out, but at the present it's worth nothing at all."

"We'll get no help from the banks," Michael said. "We not only have nothing to offer for collateral, we're still in debt to the doctor and hospital."

Something clicked in Rose's mind, setting off a surge

of excitement. "How do you ask for money from a bank?" she asked Michael. "Who would you talk to?"

Taken aback, Michael answered, "I don't know. There'd be a bank official of some sort, I'd imagine." He looked to Da. "Do you know who that would be?"

Da shook his head. "I've never had business with banks, so I couldn't be telling you for sure, but you're probably right, Michael. There'd be some kind of a bank official in charge of things."

"Jane Addams would know," Rose told them. "At Hull House they teach people how to understand credit and how to use banks."

"But Rosie," Michael remonstrated, "bankers don't just hand over money if you have nothing of value to put in its place."

"We have our own good minds and our own strong backs," Rose said. "We'll earn the money and pay back every cent."

"That's not enough."

Rose got to her feet. "I won't believe that unless I hear Miss Addams say those very same words herself."

"Are you going there now?" Da asked.

"As soon as I get my hat," Rose answered.

Da stood, too, and for an instant Rose could see in him the strong, young father he used to be. "Then I'll escort you, daughter," he said. "It's a fine, bright night, and there may be a few rapscallions about, stirring up mischief."

With a grateful heart Rose hugged her father, and the faint hope that had begun to grow became a strong, positive feeling. Everything would work out the way it should. She'd find a way to make it happen.

As they made the trip to Hull House, Rose felt as close to her father as she had when she was a little girl. People sat on their front stoops, enjoying the night air, and children played tag and chase around and under the streetlights. Smells of cabbage and onions and spices drifted from wide-open windows, and occasional bursts of music overrode the jangle and clank of the cable cars.

Hull House was bright with lights when they arrived, and Rose entered the classroom building, her right hand tucked inside her father's elbow.

He removed his hat and nodded at a well-dressed woman. *Expensive,* Rose thought as she took careful note of the woman's braid-trimmed brown silk dress with a brown-and-white hat to match. As the woman stepped up to greet them with a smile, Rose asked, "Please, ma'am, do you know where we can find Jane Addams?"

"Miss Addams is in Washington, D.C., on business," the woman said. Rose realized how distraught she must have looked when the woman quickly added, "My name is Edna. Is there anything *I* can do to help you?"

"We don't want to be troubling you," Da told her, and Rose could feel his arm tremble.

Rose was determined. She introduced Da and herself, then said, "Jane Addams told me that banking and credit classes are taught here, and we need to learn how to borrow money from a bank. My mother has died, and my two little sisters are still in Ireland. We have no money to send my father to get them, so we'll need to borrow some as soon as we can."

The woman glanced toward the open door of a still-lighted, empty classroom. "Come in here with me," she said. "I'm a friend of Jane Addams and a volunteer here at Hull House. I don't teach the class on financial matters, but I know enough about banking procedure to give you the information you'll need."

Soon they were seated in three wooden chairs, drawn close together, and the woman said, "When you request a loan, a banker is going to ask you what kind of collateral you have to back that loan."

"I understand that part," Rose said.

"Do you have collateral?"

Rose took a deep breath and repeated what she had told Michael. "My father, my brother, and I have good minds and strong backs. We will work to pay back every cent of the loan and every cent of the interest due on it."

For a few moments the woman was silent, and Rose couldn't stand it. She found herself pouring out the whole story about Johnny's arrest and Michael's accident—even her attempt to ask Alderman McMahan for help. Although Da squirmed uncomfortably beside her, by the time she had finished Rose felt emptied of a great weight. Nothing had been hidden, nothing excused. Let the woman make of it what she wished.

Edna studied Rose before she asked, "Do you realize that it would be impossible to get funds from a bank to help your brother?"

Rose sighed, hoping that what McMahan had told her about the Irish militant groups who would support Johnny was true. "Johnny was ever the headstrong one," she said, "and what he did was done by choice. It's Meggie and Bridget who need our help the most."

Edna nodded. "To be very honest with you both, I'm afraid any bank would also turn down your request for

156

traveling funds, but there's another avenue of help. Miss Addams has a number of wealthy friends who donate time and money to Hull House to be used for some of the people who come in need."

Da spoke up. His voice was husky and his face was red as he said, "We are not asking for charity."

"Do you have a job, Mr. Carney?" Although the words were blunt, the concern in Edna's manner softened them.

"Not at the present," he said.

"What type of work do you do?"

"I've been working as a bricklayer."

"That's difficult work."

"I catch your meaning," Da told her, "and you're right. It's a job for younger men, which is why I'm having trouble being hired."

"Since that is the case, then I . . ."

"But I've come up with a plan," Da continued. "I haven't told Rosie and my son Michael yet because I'm waiting until I can bring them good news. I've applied for a job with the city parks department as a gardener. They have no openings now, but my name's on a list, and I shall keep applying and reapplying until I'm hired, no matter how long it takes."

Rose's surprise at hearing her father's plan quickly turned to pride in him for trying to work out a way to help the family and himself.

"In Ireland, for most of my life," Da said, "I was a farmer and a good one at that. I know the soil, I know the land."

Edna smiled. "I can see that this is where your heart is."

Da smiled back. "You can truthfully say it."

"Would you have to work for the city? Would you be willing to work as a gardener at a private home?"

"I hadn't thought of private homes because I knew a city job would be secure. But I suppose *where* I work doesn't matter. What counts is that I'd be working at a job I can do well."

Edna sat quietly for a moment and seemed to be thinking. Finally, she said, "I think, Mr. Carney, we can help each other. I live on a large estate on Lake Shore Drive. The grounds are taken care of by a head gardener and two assistants. One of the young men plans to leave in two months, because he's moving to Michigan, and will have to be replaced. It's a full-time job, and the pay is two dollars a day. Here's what I suggest. If you're interested in taking the job, I'll advance what you need for the trip. You can begin work when you've returned with your younger daughters and repay me then."

Da leaned forward, and Rose could see the quick pulse thumping in his neck. "It's fine and generous you are to offer this job, and it's one I would like very much, Miss ... Miss ... I can no longer call you Edna."

My name is Mrs. Paul Ashley," Edna said.

"Fine then, Mrs. Ashley," Da went on. "As I was saying, I would like the job. I'll work hard and well, but you must understand that before I go to get my little girls I must stop a day or two in England, where my son Johnny is being held, and see to his needs. He *is* my son."

"Of course," Edna Ashley said. "If he were my son, I'd do the same."

Da stood beaming. Rose, whose heart was jumping as though it were on a string, said, "Thank you, Mrs. Ashley. We couldn't have worked this out without your

158

help." She would have loved to throw her arms about this kind, caring woman.

Mrs. Ashley wrote her address and telephone number on a sheet of paper and handed it to Da. In turn, she took his address. "I will send a messenger tomorrow morning to deliver the money you'll need for the journey."

Tucking her hand into her father's arm and giving it a squeeze, Rose leaned against his shoulder as they left the building. The excitement in his body was like the electricity that hummed through the trolley wires. "I'm so proud of you!" she said. "You'll have a job you'll like, and you'll be your old self again."

"That I will," he answered. "I just wish Maura were here. She'd be so pleased."

"She'll be pleased as well when Bridget and Meggie are safely with us." Rose's throat tightened with longing for her mother.

She turned to her father with a solemn expression. "Da, the best part is that you won't need to go to Casey's to find out if anyone is hiring. You'll stop drinking too much."

"We've talked about this before, so you'll not need to bring the topic up again," Da said. "I'll not touch another drop, Rosie, as long as I live."

"Do you promise?"

He raised his right hand as if he were taking an oath. "I do. I promise you, and I promise myself."

All the way home Rose, who was wound tightly with excitement, kept up a happy chatter, while Da, smiling, listened and nodded.

Rose could hardly wait to tell Michael what had happened, so she ran up the stairs and burst into their flat ahead of Da. She began at the beginning, not leaving out a single detail as she tried to recount every word of the conversation. At last, Rose paused for a breath and flung herself into a chair. "Da's going to love working with the land again."

She looked around, and to her amazement there was no sign of her father. "Where's Da?" she asked Michael.

He shrugged. "He didn't come in with you."

"Then where . . . ?"

Rose ran down the stairs and out onto the walk, but there was no sign of her father.

Mr. O'Brien, returning late from work, materialized from the darkness. "If you're looking for your father, Miss Carney," he said, "I passed him down the block."

"Going to Casey's?"

"It looked that way."

"Thank you," Rose said. Slowly, each step aching and heavy, she climbed the stairs and entered the parlor and sank into a chair.

"Da's gone to Casey's," she told Michael. "I should have known. He can't be trusted to go for the girls. How will we be able to hand over to him Mrs. Ashley's loan?"

"I'll be off these crutches in less than a month," Michael offered. "I'll get our sisters."

Rose shook her head. "Think how frightened Meggie and Bridget must be—their mother gone and no one coming to get them. Someone has to go *now*."

"Da's in no shape to do it."

"That I know! But who else is there who can go?" Rose struck the arms of the chair with her fists. "Da promised never to touch another drop again, Michael!

He promised! And I believed him, but he couldn't keep his word for thirty minutes!"

As she got to her feet Michael held out a restraining arm. "Don't go after him, Rosie. It hurts his pride."

Impatiently, Rose brushed her brother's arm away. "I have no intention of trying to coax him out of Casey's. That wouldn't solve a thing."

"And neither will sitting here agonizing about Da's problem." Juggling his crutches, Michael struggled to his feet. "I'm going to bed, Rosie. Why don't you? You look so tired."

"I am tired," Rose answered, "but I'm so tired I'm past sleep. I just want to sit here and think awhile about what to do next."

Michael's voice was hopeful. "Do you have any ideas?"

"None."

Rose didn't remember closing her eyes, so she was startled when she awoke to hear Da fumbling his way through the front doorway.

As he closed the door he spotted Rose, focusing on her in surprise. "Still up?" he asked cheerfully. "Ah, then it's not as late as I thought it might be."

"Why did you go to Casey's, Da?" Rose asked.

"I had to tell the boys our good fortune," he answered. A wheedling note came into his voice. "You understand, don't you, Rosie? What kind of a friend would I be if I didn't share the news and say good-bye to all the boys?"

Rose slowly got to her feet, exhausted and ill. "You promised you wouldn't touch another drop. You promised me."

Da straightened his shoulders, struggling to reach his full height. He patted Rose's shoulder clumsily and announced with all the confidence he could muster, "I intend to keep that promise, Rosie girl. Never fear. Tonight I had to say good-bye to my friends, but from tomorrow on I'll keep my promise."

Rose helped her father to bed, then went to her own room, closing the door. In the moonlight-flooded room she quickly changed to her nightgown and crawled into bed, the gold locket warm on her chest. There was no hope left, she thought. None at all.

# CHAPTER SEVENTEEN

❖ ❖ ❖

KATE arrived at the store the next afternoon, one little boy in hand, the other in her arms. "I couldn't wait to see you!" she whispered. "Tim told me about Johnny's arrest. Those stupid, foolish boys! Oh, Rosie, I'm so sorry!"

"Shhh," Rose said, glancing toward Mrs. Sweeney's back. "We're not supposed to entertain friends. Besides, what's done is done."

Kate lowered her voice to a murmur. "At least all the news wasn't bad. I heard about Mrs. Ashley and the loan and the job!"

"She told you?" Rose asked in amazement.

"No, no. One of my friends was working in the next room. She overheard. You don't mind, do you?" Kate suddenly pulled a skirt from the nearest rack and in a louder voice said, "Yes, it's a lovely shade of blue, but I came to look at clothing for my little boys."

Rose saw Mrs. Sweeney turn away, offering her help to a newly arrived customer. She led Kate to the children's clothing section of the store and said, "I was so happy, Kate. I thought Mrs. Ashley was the answer to our problem. Da even solemnly promised me that he wouldn't take another drink." She choked back a sob, struggling to keep her composure. "But when we arrived home he didn't even come in the house with me. While I was telling Michael our good news, Da went straight to Casey's."

Kate's eyes were huge and dark. "Oh, Rosie, what are you going to do?"

"I don't know yet," Rose told her. "I honestly don't know."

"There has to be an answer."

"If there is I haven't found it."

"Don't give up. Who knows what might turn up?"

Mrs. Sweeney joined them, asking Kate, "Have you found something for those dear little boys?"

"Not exactly," Kate answered and nodded at Rose, "but I do thank you, miss, for your helpfulness." She left the store, and Rose began to wait on another customer.

During the rest of the day Rose kept her mind on her work, not allowing herself to dwell on her problems. Until last night she had refused to despair, positive that there would always be solutions, but she had done everything possible, and the right answers hadn't come.

As Rose and the Sweeneys left the store, Mr. Sweeney carefully locking the door behind them, Rose blurted out,

"If I went to Ireland to get my sisters, could I have my job back when I returned home?"

In surprise, Mrs. Sweeney answered, "We'd have to replace you, Rose. There'd be no other way. We can't train a new employee and then fire her when you get back."

"Of course," Rose said. "I shouldn't have asked."

"We heard what happened to your brother Johnny, and we're sorry. We'll be doubly sorry if you leave us."

"I won't," Rose said. "It was a foolish question."

Mr. Sweeney broke in. "It seems to me this is a father's job. Is there any reason why your father can't go after the children?"

Rose evaded an answer. "Here comes my trolley," she said as she began to run across the street. "I'll see you in the morning."

When Rose was two doors from her house she easily recognized the figure seated on the steps. Her heart quickened, and so did her footsteps, as she approached Tim.

He slowly got to his feet and came to meet her as she reached the walk.

"Kate told me everything that happened," Tim said.

"It's kind of you to care," Rose murmured.

"Kind of me to care!" Tim repeated her words loudly as he grabbed her shoulders. "I'm not being kind! I'm going out of my mind because I do care so much about you, Rosie!" He lowered his voice and dropped his hands to his sides. "I take the blame for all the unhappiness you've been caused by Johnny's arrest. The loss of my friend—oh, Rosie, there's so much I feel responsible for. I don't blame you for hating me."

Rose recognized the terrible hurt in Tim's eyes and realized she should have seen that he had been mourning,

165

too. Her love for him growing even stronger, she whispered, "I don't hate you"; but Tim, intent on what he had come to say, went on.

"You won't have to worry about sending your father to Ireland, because I'll be going with him."

"You?" Rose gasped.

"Yes, and I'll never let him out of my sight. We'll stop in England to see what is being done for Johnny and what still can be done, and then we'll get your little sisters and bring them home."

"But your fare will be expensive. I can't ask you to spend that much money."

Tim shook his head. "Let's say that the alderman owed me a few favors and was glad to help out."

Rose took a step backward. "You won't be smuggling illegal funds, too, will you?"

He flinched at her words, and Rose saw the hurt she had caused. "No smuggling. You have my word on it. Please believe me, Rosie, I'll be going only to help your father . . . and you. I've already talked to him and to Michael. You'll be interested to know that Michael put himself in charge of the money that was sent this morning."

Rose sighed with relief. "I trust you, Tim, and I believe you. It's just that after all that has happened, I didn't see how things could ever go right again."

Tim's look was wistful as he said, "I'm glad I could put your mind at ease, Rosie. Now I'll be going and won't be any more bother to you."

"No!" Rose reached out and clasped one of his hands, clinging as though she'd never let go. "I lied to you," she said. "I told you that I hated you, and I don't. I never did. I couldn't. I spoke only out of anger. Oh, Tim, I love you with all my heart!"

For an instant his eyes brightened, but warily he held back. "You may be angry with me again, Rosie. I have my way of looking at things, and you have your way. I can tell you right now I won't change." He paused before he added, "And since fair is fair, I'd never expect you to change just to suit me."

"My mother and father didn't always see things eye to eye," Rose told him, "but they loved each other deeply, and that's what counts."

"Are you saying . . . ?"

"Yes," she interrupted. "I knew that coming to America would change things, but I didn't know it would change *me*. I'm not the girl I was in Ireland. I'm a grown woman now, and I know this for sure. I love you, Tim."

He smiled broadly and took her in his arms. "And I love you, Rosie. I always will."

Even though there'd been sorrow, there had also been joy. The future with Tim held a beautiful promise, and Rose intended to make the most of it.

# ABOUT ELLIS ISLAND

❖ ❖ ❖

ELLIS ISLAND, called by many the "gateway to America," represents a landmark of America's rich cultural heritage. Four out of ten Americans have family who passed through this important place as immigrants.

From 1892 to 1954 the millions of immigrants who entered the United States through Ellis Island first saw a massive wooden building with a blue slate roof and ornamental towers. In 1897 this structure mysteriously burned to the ground. Fortunately, no one was injured, but thousands of immigration records were lost.

A new building was constructed and opened in 1900—an impressive edifice of red-and-yellow brick, where during the next ten years more than 6 million people were processed. The majority of these immigrants came from Italy, Russia, and Austria-Hungary; but there were many who came from England, Ireland, Germany, and the

Scandinavian countries; and some came from Canada, the West Indies, Poland, Greece, Portugal, and Armenia.

Entry to the United States at Ellis Island wasn't easy. Immigrants faced examinations and inspections and—because of outbreaks of public fear that these individuals might not be able to support themselves—those with poor health or physical handicaps were returned to the countries from which they came. The complex and confusing entry to the United States was initially made even more difficult for the immigrants because they often did not know English or understand the value of dollars, and they were cheated by money changers, baggage handlers, and those who sold train tickets. In early 1902 President Theodore Roosevelt hired William Williams, a New York attorney, to clean out the graft and corruption, and he did.

For many years the Ellis Island buildings were deserted, but in 1980 President Ronald Reagan invited Lee Iacocca, chairman of the Chrysler Corporation, to orchestrate the renovation of both the Ellis Island immigration station and the Statue of Liberty through public donations. Over 20 million people responded with gifts totaling over 300 million dollars. Today Ellis Island is a beautiful museum, preserving the stories of its immigrants for history.

Three of my four grandparents were immigrants to this country, so writing the Ellis Island books has been especially meaningful to me.

# ABOUT THE AUTHOR

JOAN LOWERY NIXON is the acclaimed author of more than eighty fiction and nonfiction books for children and young adults. She is a three-time winner of the Mystery Writers of America Edgar Award and the recipient of many Children's Choice Awards. Her popular books for young adults include *High Trail to Danger,* and its companion novel, *A Deadly Promise,* the bestselling Orphan Train Quartet, for which she received two Golden Spur Awards, the Hollywood Daughters trilogy, and *Land of Hope,* the first volume of the Ellis Island Trilogy. She is currently working on volume three of the Ellis Island books.

Mrs. Nixon and her husband live in Houston, Texas.